Luscious

OTHER BOOKS BY LEXI BLAKE

EROTIC ROMANCE

Masters and Mercenaries
The Dom Who Loved Me
The Men With The Golden Cuffs
A Dom Is Forever
On Her Master's Secret Service
Sanctum: A Masters and Mercenaries Novella
Love and Let Die
Unconditional: A Masters and Mercenaries Novella
Dungeon Royale
Dungeon Games: A Masters and Mercenaries Novella
A View to a Thrill
Cherished: A Masters and Mercenaries Novella
You Only Love Twice
Luscious: Masters and Mercenaries~Topped
Adored: A Masters and Mercenaries Novella
Master No, Coming August 4, 2015

Masters Of Ménage (by Shayla Black and Lexi Blake)
Their Virgin Captive
Their Virgin's Secret
Their Virgin Concubine
Their Virgin Princess
Their Virgin Hostage
Their Virgin Secretary
Their Virgin Mistress

The Perfect Gentlemen (by Shayla Black and Lexi Blake)
Scandal Never Sleeps, Coming Soon August 18, 2015
Seduction in Session, Coming January 5, 2016

URBAN FANTASY

Thieves
Steal the Light
Steal the Day
Steal the Moon
Steal the Sun
Steal the Night
Ripper
Addict, Coming September 22, 2015

Luscious

Masters and Mercenaries, Book 8.25
Lexi Blake

Luscious
Masters and Mercenaries, Book 8.25
Lexi Blake

Published by DLZ Entertainment LLC

Print ISBN: 978-1-937608-45-3

Sign up for Lexi Blake's newsletter
and be entered to win a $25 gift certificate
to the bookseller of your choice.

Join us for news, fun, and exclusive content
including free short stories.

There's a new contest every month!

Go to www.LexiBlake.net to subscribe.

PROLOGUE

Arlington, Virginia

Macon Miles sat up and it took a moment for him to realize that the ringing in his head was actually the doorbell. How much had he had to drink? His stomach turned as he took in his surroundings. He was in his shitty one-bedroom on the couch Elise had decided she didn't want because the dog had pissed on it or something. Her dog, of course. She'd kept the dog but not the couch or him.

He looked down. Six months and he still checked. He would have thought he would be used to it, but every time he woke up, he had to check.

Yep, still only had one fucking leg. One and a quarter. Maybe a little more, but not quite a third. God, he was a kid counting his age in quarters and halves except he was doing it with what was left of his limbs. One and what? Something less than half, more than a fourth. Yeah, that described his leg all right. Maybe if he'd been better at math he wouldn't have gotten his leg blown off.

There was a volley of knocks, but he slumped back down on the couch. Whoever it was could go away. It was probably one of the neighbors trying to sell him some meth. Yeah, it was that kind of place.

He stared up at his ceiling and tried to find some semblance of will.

Will to do anything. Will to get off the couch. Will to breathe. Will to fucking live.

Nope. That had apparently been blown to shit with his leg. He'd left his willpower in Afghanistan along with his limb. He laughed. Life and limb. He'd promised he would give it all for his country and he had. His leg had been sacrificed to the almighty IED.

And his wife had sacrificed, too. She'd sacrificed their marriage, her morals, her dignity, very likely any chance at future orgasms because he knew her new man and he was a selfish asswipe.

Unfortunately, he was also Macon's oldest brother.

He closed his eyes. The banging had finally stopped. Maybe he could find some peace, or at least another bottle of whiskey.

When he went to get the whiskey, he should also get some sugar and eggs.

That thought made him sit up. *Pastry Chef Wars* was coming on tonight. They were all self-centered douchebags, but he kind of liked the show. Okay. He was pretty obsessed with it. One of the boxes Elise had shipped to his new place had come from their rarely used kitchen. She sure as hell wouldn't deign to cook, and he'd been getting his ass blown up halfway across the world, so the kitchen tabletop appliances they'd received for their wedding were mostly unused.

One day, in between horrifically painful PT sessions, he'd opened his mother's old recipe book. He hadn't really known the woman. She'd died long before he had memories at all, but his stepmother, in an uncommon fit of sentimentality, had saved her recipe book. It was a notebook written in his mother's own careful hand.

He'd opened it and felt some connection to that woman who had given birth to him all those years before. He touched the pages and read the words. The first recipe had been for chocolate cream pie, and he'd smiled when he got to the last ingredient. *Love.* She'd drawn a heart beside the word.

His mother's recipes always included love. He didn't have any of that now, but he did like playing around with desserts. He'd been surprised to find he was good at it.

If his Army buddies could see him now… Not that he would let them.

He thought briefly about Ronnie's sister. Ronnie Rowe had been the new kid. He could still vaguely remember meeting him the day he'd

8

joined Macon's team. Ronnie had been so green. The kid had thrown up after his first firefight. He hadn't really known much about Rowe until that day…

His sister kept calling, but he couldn't talk to her. Not yet. Maybe never. He'd failed so terrifically that he didn't want Ronnie's sister to ever meet him. He wondered if she looked like Ronnie. He'd been a tall goofball with red hair and freckles.

And then he'd been nothing but a body on the ground. He'd been nothing at all and Macon had been left alone. Sometimes he woke up in the middle of the night and Ronnie's body was still there, right beside him, blank eyes staring up and reminding him that he was the only one left.

Sometimes he thought he should have let them take him. A bullet to the brain might have been the easier way out than this slow, pathetic march.

The sound of the door scraping open brought Macon out of his thoughts, and his heart rate tripled. He looked around the room. Where the fuck was his leg? No. Screw the leg. He needed his gun. Where had that gone?

And where was his damn death wish when he needed it?

"Macon? Don't shoot me."

Macon stilled. He hadn't heard that voice in years. No. He couldn't do it. The last thing he needed was this. He was freaking dreaming and his brother was going to make him feel like shit. Not the oldest one. Not the one who had run out with Macon's wife. No. This was worse. The voice he heard was Adam, the brother he'd wronged himself. The last person in the world he wanted to see was Adam because Adam was the only one he couldn't hate.

He often wondered if his mother had stayed alive, would she have allowed things to go so wrong? Did she look down and weep because her family was so very broken?

"Hey."

He opened his eyes and was suddenly really sure this wasn't a dream. His brother was standing in front of him, dressed like some fucking movie star and looking years younger than Macon felt. "How did you get in? You should leave."

Adam grinned as though he hadn't expected less. "You have serious issues with security, little brother. I picked that lock in no time flat. This place is a one-star roach motel. I don't even think most roaches would stay here."

He was wrong about that. Macon had to beat the disgusting fuckers back constantly. Adam. God. His brother was standing right in front of him and Macon had to wonder if he hadn't come for revenge. Had he come to see how far his brother had fallen?

Did it matter? His first instinct had been to tell him to fuck off, but now that he was standing right here, he kind of wanted to beg him to stay. He and Adam had been closest in age. Alan hadn't had time for little brothers, but Adam had always been patient and gentle with him. Even when it pissed off their dad because brothers were supposed to fight for position, not treat each other like pussies who couldn't handle a punch.

Fuck it all. He didn't want to fight anymore. Every minute of every day seemed like a fight and now Adam was here and Macon was five again. He wanted his brother to make things better.

He'd lost that right.

Adam sighed as he took in the room. "This is significantly worse than your dorm room. And what is that smell?"

It could be anything. He'd gone nose blind two weeks into his new life. He'd gone from hospitals and their antiseptic smells to this place.

He tried to straighten up. God, he wished he'd brushed his teeth. His mouth still tasted like cheap whiskey. He might have one shot at this. He'd nearly died and the one regret he had was never telling Adam how he felt. Adam might have come here for revenge and Macon would give it to him. He deserved it. Macon had been a shit and anything Adam wanted to dole out would be nothing compared to the hate he felt for himself. But he owed Adam one thing, and now that he was standing right here, Macon was determined to pay up.

"I'm sorry, Adam. You should know I think every single day about what I did to you." His brother was into alternative lifestyles, to say the least. When he'd gotten kicked out of the Army for breaking Don't Ask, Don't Tell, Macon had been pressured into shunning him. He hadn't, not all the way, but he also hadn't fought for his brother. He hadn't stood up for Adam the way Adam would have stood up for him. "I tried...no, I didn't try hard enough. I should have walked away. I should have told them to fuck themselves. You and Jake are a really great couple. You should be allowed to be happy."

Adam groaned and looked around, seeming to try to find a clean place to sit. He remained standing. "Dude, we're not lovers. I'm straight. Jake's straight. I've never once touched that man's junk and I never will. We share."

"Share? Like love and stuff?" It didn't compute.

A long sigh came from his brother's mouth and Macon was pretty sure he was getting Adam's "dumbass said what" face. "Did the IED blow up your IQ? We share a wife. We've shared women for years. It was what we were doing that got us kicked out of the Army. We were discovered with a superior officer between us. A female superior, who also happened to have caught the eye of a general. The general had not taken kindly to the infraction. Dad is the one who told you I was gay. Here's a surprise. Dad lies."

"There's nothing wrong with being gay. It's natural." He'd briefly tried that argument with his father and Alan, but Elise had shut him down. She'd wanted a house off base and the only way to get it was with help from dear old Dad. Macon had tried to convince her to tough it out, but she'd cried and cried and he'd sold his brother out in the end because it was easier to let Adam go than to fight it out with everyone else.

He'd been a fucking coward.

"It's not considered natural in our family, but I'm glad you see it that way. You always did have a mind of your own." Adam finally cleared off a space on the coffee table and sat down in front of Macon. "You called to let me know the important stuff. You called to let me know Dad was sick. How much trouble did you get in for doing that?"

"It doesn't matter. The bastard keeps holding on. His remission seems to be long term." The last conversation he'd had with his father, the old man had told him to suck it up, of course Elise preferred Alan. Alan was more of a man than Macon was.

He hadn't talked to his family since then.

"You risked a lot to call me, but you didn't bother to give me a ring about nearly dying? Oh, there was the drunk dial of two nights ago that brought me here, but I could have used a sober heads-up. You're lucky I kept the same cell number all these years."

Shit. He'd done that? Embarrassment flashed through his system. "Fuck. I didn't realize I'd called. I kind of lost track of the phone. I shouldn't have called you at all."

"Yeah, you should have. You should have called me while you were

11

at Ramstein. You should have called me when you got home and realized your wife was fucking big brother and they had both screwed you over. What the hell are you doing in this rat hole?"

He'd forgotten that Adam could play the fatherly role from time to time. "I can't afford anything else. Dad cut me off and my Army severance isn't much. Elise stayed married to me long enough to take half the insurance settlement I got on my leg." TSGLI paid out a hundred grand for traumatic injuries. Elise had taken fifty thousand and then also shared her maxed out credit card bills with him. She was a giver.

"How are you getting to rehab?"

"Bus." He was still wobbly on the damn prosthetic. He'd fallen more than once and the humiliation always burned through him.

Adam sighed. "You're coming home with me. What of this crap do I need to pack? And where's your damn leg? Shouldn't it be close to you?"

His brother got up and started walking around the apartment, poking into everything. Macon was ashamed of how messy he'd let the place get. He'd been taught to be neat, that everything had a place. "Adam, I can't go with you."

Adam turned. "Why not?"

He couldn't think of a single reason why. Not one. He hated his life. He didn't have a family anymore.

He could have a fresh start. Maybe in Dallas he wouldn't sit around and drink all day. Maybe if he wasn't constantly reminded of everything he'd lost, he could build something new. Did he even want that?

Adam came to stand in front of him, placing a hand on his shoulder. It was the first time he'd been connected to his brother in years. "That old life is gone, Macon. Unless you want to try to win her back…"

"Not in a million years. I can't stand the thought of that woman. Or Alan. Or…god, I hate them all, Adam. I fucking hate them all. It eats me up inside until I don't want to do anything but remember how much I hate them."

"Then come to Dallas and we'll start over. I have a son. I promise you can't be around him and keep all that hate in your gut. You can stay in the guesthouse if you like. It's really just a house. When we moved we bought two lots and kept one of the old houses while we built the dream house. Now we keep it for family. Jake's got a massive family and it's really easier to not share a house with all of them. You can stay there long term and I'll find a physical therapist in the neighborhood."

Adam had a baby? A son? He had a nephew? He couldn't let his nephew see him like this. He had to clean up. He had to sober up. Damn. He did have a family. Adam was offering him one.

"Macon?"

Macon focused again. "Why? Why would you help me?"

Adam sighed and leaned forward. "Because you're my brother. Because I learned a long time ago that life is way too short to hold grudges or to waste it on hating things we can't change. I would like my son to know one of his uncles. I would like to be a brother to you and I would definitely like to avoid having to bury you, and I'm fairly certain that's where all this is heading if you don't come with me."

A single moment played out in his head, the memory as fresh as if it had happened yesterday. He'd been standing in the doorway, watching his big brothers getting in the car to go away to school. He couldn't go to school, but Alan and Adam were going to learn how to be soldiers, like their dad. They would be gone for a long time. They were going to something called boarding school.

Just when he thought they would leave without another word, Adam had bolted back and he'd hugged Macon. "I'll miss you."

They weren't supposed to hug, but it felt right. He held on to his brother until their father broke them up and hustled Adam to the car.

He'd been left behind, but Adam wasn't leaving him behind this time. Despite everything that had happened, Adam was here.

He could stay and let hate eat up his whole fucking life or he could start over.

"My prosthetic is in the bathroom, but I might have used it to smash the mirror, so you should probably watch out for that."

Adam shook his head. "You're seeing a shrink, too."

He would if Adam told him to. It was far past time to listen to someone who had it together. "And I don't need to bring much."

Some clothes and one book. His mother's recipe book.

Maybe it would come in handy.

* * * *

Sarah Allyson Jones stared down at the headstones. One was fresh, the other only months old. She'd spent all the cash she had left on those two slabs of marble and concrete.

Sunshine washed over the graves. It was a gorgeous Georgia day and that seemed like the greatest insult of all. The grass was green, forsythia in full bloom. Everywhere she looked there were peaceful plants coming to life. The cemetery was a contrast—a garden of green for the dead.

She wanted rain. She wanted the plants to rot and the sky to fall around her.

She wanted to go back to the woman she'd been before Ronnie's death. No. Before her mother's illness. Had it really been so long since she'd laughed and teased and felt like she had a future?

"Your mother was a kind woman," a soft voice said. When Sarah turned around she saw the preacher standing there. Reverend Alton was a nice man. She'd been going to his church since she was a teenager. "The last few months of her life were an aberration."

The last few months of her life had been all about pain and lies. Agony from the cancer eating her lungs and lies from the Army. Her mother had sent her only son off to fight for his country and all she'd gotten back was a pine box and lies about how he died.

Ronnie hadn't been her blood. Sarah had been a foster kid who won the lottery. She'd been thirteen when Carla Rowe agreed to foster her long enough to find a permanent home. A few months had turned into years, and she'd found a better home than the misery she had before.

How could it all be gone? How could they be here? Had those years of happiness been a momentary respite? Would her life be about misery again?

"She was angry after Ronnie died." Somehow she felt the need to defend her foster mother. She touched the arch of the gravestone, feeling the cool of the stone beneath her palm. She prayed there was peace there for Carla and that she was with her son again.

Sweet, goofy Ronnie, her brother. He'd been kind and smart and at times she'd had to protect him from bullies when they were in school. After high school, they'd both worked around town, trying to save money for college. Even then her mother's health had been failing. She couldn't leave their small town, worried something would happen to Carla Rowe. Finally, eighteen months before, Ronnie had made the decision to go into the Army. He'd been twenty-four with no real prospects in sight. It had been hard to imagine him in the Army, but then he'd come home and he'd been a soldier. He'd put on muscle and gained confidence. He'd gone in because he didn't have the money for college and now he was dead.

Reverend Alton put a hand on Ronnie's stone. "He was a good son. A good man. I can't tell you why the lord chose to call him home so soon."

She didn't need platitudes. "I don't think God did this."

Unfortunately, she was fairly certain it hadn't gone down the way the Army claimed it did either. They were evasive. The reports on her brother's death were lacking in detail and the one person who had been there wouldn't speak to her.

"Sarah, your mother wouldn't want to hear the bitterness in your voice."

Sarah stood up. "My mother was the one who asked me to find out what happened. It was her dying wish."

"You want to give up everything you have? You've already spent your savings on private investigators and lawyers."

She'd spent everything. She'd already had to sell the house to pay the bills attached to her mom's long fight. The money the Army insurance had paid out went to the same place. She didn't have anything left. "I have to honor her wish."

The reverend sighed. "No, you don't."

"Seriously? A reverend is telling me to deny a woman her dying wish? That doesn't sound very godly."

"God is kinder than we make him out to be, Sarah. Your mother wasn't thinking straight. She was in pain and on drugs to manage it. She wouldn't want you to endanger your whole future."

She had no future. Her chance to go to college was blown. She was almost twenty-six and she'd spent much of the last five years nursing her mother and working dead-end jobs to try to help pay the never-ending medical bills. It was the very lack of opportunity in their tiny town that had sent Ronnie into the Army. He'd sent back every bit of pay he could spare. Not that it had mattered. It was all over now and she'd thought she'd feel some semblance of relief. Instead, she was left with this aching hole that nothing could fill.

Maybe if she found the truth, her mother could rest easier.

"Sarah?" the reverend said. "Sarah, you're too emotional to make a decision like this. Come back to the parish house. You can stay with us for a while. Come back and sit in the nursery and hold some of the babies. It will make you feel better. In a few months, you'll be in a better place to make a decision about your life."

She'd already made her decision. The money had run out so now it was up to her to do her own investigating.

She was going to find Macon Miles and when she did, she would find out how her brother had died. And if he had anything to do with it…well, she would take care of that, too.

CHAPTER ONE

Dallas, TX
Two months later

Macon watched the new girl. He couldn't help himself. She was luscious. Like a chocolate soufflé. She would require very careful handling in order to bring her to fruition. One wrong move and a woman like that would fold, wilting or falling away, or simply telling him to fuck off.

He really didn't want her to tell him to fuck off.

Ally. Allyson Jones. She had dark hair and a curvy figure that filled out her black slacks and white dress shirt in a way no one else on the waitstaff managed. She bent over, collecting the menus. That was the singular juiciest backside he'd ever seen. It was fucking spectacular, and he could feel his cock hardening.

It was not helpful to his current work situation, but he still couldn't force his eyes to move. It was like they were laser focused on that lush ass.

He moved the pastry blender over and over, forcing the ingredients to mix into something new. Butter, flour, sugar, shortening, salt, and ice water. His perfect piecrust. Simple and yet so complex since he'd learned it required something beyond merely following the recipe. There was a harmony required most people never figured out, a certain Zen that came with giving over to the dish, allowing it to be what it would.

"Don't let that sit too long." Timothy Gage looked down his patrician nose at the bowl. "We have reservations for a hundred tonight. If that crust isn't perfect, I'll see you go back to washing dishes."

Macon took a deep breath and forced himself not to correct his obnoxiously pretentious boss. He'd never washed dishes. When he'd been hired at Top, he'd been brought in as a garde-manger, prepping salads and helping with small plates. That had lasted two weeks. Then one day the chef's brother had walked in. Ian Taggart was a massive slab of muscle with a taste for lemons. Timothy didn't do requests. He was an artiste, or at least that's what he called himself. He was mostly an asshole who took himself way too seriously. Sean Taggart, the man who owned Top, had tried to talk his brother into being reasonable. Macon had quickly made a lemon pudding.

He'd moved from salads to assistant pastry chef that day, and he was also Big Tag's hookup. The big guy's wife had been pregnant at the time and mad about coconut. He'd made coconut cookies, cream pies, and cakes for the lovely Charlotte.

It was good to be needed. It was good to make something that made someone else happy.

"That is one hot piece of ass." Timothy leaned against the wall, his eyes on Ally.

There were times he really didn't like the man. All the time, really. He was full of himself, but he was also trained by some super-fancy school in Paris. Sean had introduced him as a big deal and explained that Macon could learn a lot from him. So far he'd really learned that Timothy liked to duck work and take all the credit, and he drank on the job.

Ally looked up and her dark eyes caught on his. He hoped he wasn't staring like a crazy stalker guy, but it was hard to look away. She smiled and joked and he could still feel the aura of loss that surrounded her. He wanted to know what made her seem so sad at times, like there was a wall between her and the world. He wanted to tell her she didn't need that wall. It was a stupid idea. He couldn't take care of himself much less anyone else, so he'd kept his distance.

Still, since the moment she'd walked through the doors, he hadn't been able to stop thinking about her.

18

She gathered the menus close to her chest as she started for the door. She stopped in front of the pastry station. The barest hint of a smile crossed her full lips. "What's on for tonight?"

Tim stepped up. "Citrus tarts and a mango sorbet. But if you like I could whip up something chocolate for you. I know the staff tends to have a limited palate. I'll fix that right up for you, sweetheart."

Ally frowned and looked back at Macon. "Well, it looks good anyway. See you later."

Macon nodded her way and then turned to Timothy. "Is there a reason you insulted her?"

Timothy waved him off. "Like she knows what a palate is. Had I really known who I would be working with here, I would have stayed in Europe." He took a sip of coffee that Macon knew was drowned in whiskey. "The whole place is full of washed-up idiots. Taggart has too soft a heart to really make it in this business. He's a brilliant chef. He simply doesn't have a proper staff around him. It's one thing to use his Army buddies to wash dishes. It's another to pretend they can actually cook."

Yes, this was what he got to listen to. It was so much better when Timothy worked on what he considered proper desserts and he left Macon alone to prepare the secondary. Unfortunately for tonight, the mango sorbet was already done, so he got to listen to Timothy's rants.

He sucked it down. He wasn't about to fuck up this job. He owed Adam too much. Adam had introduced him to Sean. Adam had gotten him this job. He couldn't lose his temper.

He went back to his crust.

Timothy drained his mug and slapped Macon on the shoulder. "You finish that up. I'm going to go deal with a problem I'm having."

He stepped out and Macon could breathe again. He let the sounds of the kitchen wash over him. He loved it here. With the singular exception of Timothy, he got along with everyone. Sean Taggart liked to hire vets. Chef Taggart was a former Green Beret and his kitchen staff came from all the arms of service. The sous-chef was a former SEAL, the saucier a former Air Force pilot. The line chefs were all Marines. Even the sommelier had spent time in the Coast Guard. Only Timothy and a few of the servers were civilians.

He fit in here. He wasn't the only scarred fuck-up.

His life had taken on a pleasing rhythm. Wake up, exercise with his brother and Jake, lunch with his sister-in-law, who asked an insane amount of questions, work, and sleep. He had PT three days a week and saw the shrink twice. He was getting comfortable telling Kai Ferguson things he'd never told another person.

The only problem was Kai thought he was holding back and he was. There was one thing he couldn't tell anyone. Not ever. He would take it to his grave.

He shoved the thoughts aside and concentrated on the individual crusts.

"You coming out with us tonight?" Eric Vail's white apron was still pristine at this point in prep. The sous-chef was a lean man of roughly forty, with a jagged scar running from above his right eye to his jawline. He also was the best freaking chef short of the big boss. Eric's sea bass rocked Macon's world.

Macon had decided that men who'd been forced to live on MREs for most of their life took food seriously.

"I'm going to close tonight." He liked closing on Sundays. Yes, it took longer because they weren't open on Mondays, so he ended up helping Sean with the accounting. He liked it because he was learning how to run a business. Once he'd offered to help with the books, Sean had been thrilled to teach him. He helped with accounting and payroll. Sean's wife, Grace, had spent hours teaching him how to use the accounting software. He loved baking, but he also loved the sense that he had a hand in the working of the business.

Eric shook his head. "You are crazy, my brother. I'll drink some tequila for you. Or maybe not since I saw that you're closing with the lovely Ally. It has not escaped my notice that you watch her."

"I'm not stalking her or anything." Not really. He just liked the way she moved when she didn't think anyone was watching. After close, they would turn on some music and she'd move to it, her feet finding a rhythm as she mouthed the words to the songs she knew.

Eric's emerald green eyes rolled. "I didn't say that. I said you obviously have a thing for her. I think you should ask her out."

He wasn't so sure about that. "I'm not in a place to take care of a girlfriend."

Eric frowned and leaned in. "If you give a crap about that girl, maybe you should rethink your position."

"What does that mean?"

"I've been talking to Deena." Eric was cozy with the hostess. She was a pretty blonde who didn't seem to give a shit that Eric was scarred. She beamed when he walked in the room. "No one knows where Ally lives. A couple of the guys have asked and she puts them off with that smile of hers."

He wasn't stupid. The waitstaff was tight. They watched out for each other. Even after a few weeks, someone should have been to Ally's place. Eric was right about that smile though. When she did smile, it kind of lit up the room. "Maybe she's staying with a friend."

"Or maybe she's staying in that piece of shit Ford that's always parked down the street on the nights she works. I walked by after Deena mentioned it. There are a couple of blankets and pillows in the back. I'm telling you if you like the girl, you better make your claim because someone's going to take an interest sooner or later. The minute Sean Taggart figures out one of his employees is living in her car, he'll take over. We don't call it Top for nothing, brother." Eric put a hand on his shoulder. "You have some time. Figure it out."

Top was a play on words. It hadn't taken long to figure that out. His brother had explained that most of his friends, including Chef Taggart, were into the BDSM lifestyle. They played around for the most part, but there wasn't a single one of those men who wouldn't take responsibility for a female in need. They would step in and help because it was the right thing to do.

He kind of liked his brother's friends.

Eric walked away and Macon was left with a dilemma.

He wasn't good for Ally. There was no question about that. He was only now starting to deal with his responsibilities, and taking on another one might not be the best idea. He was kind of toxic.

But wasn't toxic better than homeless? She was sweet. She was sad. She worked her butt off every night and he'd noticed she helped her coworkers when they struggled. When the front was slow, she came back to the kitchen and tried to help them. Shouldn't someone watch out for her? He'd heard she didn't have any family left. She always turned down going out at night, preferring to work late. Maybe she was trying to save money for a place of her own.

He didn't like the thought of her sleeping in her car. It was dangerous.

The guesthouse had two bedrooms. His brother's guesthouse was bigger than most people's actual houses. Adam had done well for himself. Adam wouldn't stop him from bringing a stray home. Hell, they would likely welcome her with open arms. The Dean-Miles family liked to take in strays.

He finished with the crusts and went to wash his hands. Maybe it was time to ask Ally a few questions.

Maybe it was time to give a shit about someone other than himself.

* * * *

Ally dropped off the new menus. They changed nightly because Sean Taggart liked to use fresh ingredients. Top was farm to table. He negotiated with local farms for whatever he could, and as far as Ally could tell he was one hell of a chef. She'd been raised on whatever her mom had a coupon for, but she'd discovered she really liked sea bass and polenta, and god she could eat risotto all day.

And Macon's pastries. Oh, Timothy the Ass took credit, but she watched Macon work. Macon made the fluffiest crust, the richest chocolate mousse.

He was also the damn dreamiest man she'd ever seen, and she wasn't a woman who used the word dreamiest lightly.

In the few weeks she'd worked at Top, she would swear she'd gained ten pounds. After service was over, staff got to eat. She'd had some of the best food of her life here. She'd also had some really good times. She'd thought she only ever fit in with her mom and Ronnie, but this place was starting to feel like home.

"Hey, you. I heard we're going to Deep Ellum after work tonight." Deena took the menus and placed them in the basket by the hostess station. She was an infinitely competent woman in her early thirties, with a ready smile and a warm personality. She kept the front of house running like clockwork. "Tell me you're coming with us. We need to dance."

Oddly, the idea of going clubbing held no appeal. She was young and single and had no ties to anyone, and yet all she wanted to do was have a place to go to with a TV and a warm bed and a Macon Miles to cuddle up against.

Damn it. She couldn't think that way. Macon was the target. Macon was the only one who could tell her what really happened to her brother.

22

The report didn't make sense. She knew the Army could cover up deaths, and she was sure that was what happened with Ronnie.

Had Macon killed her brother? Somehow she didn't think so. She certainly didn't want to believe it. She'd walked into Top with the full intention of confronting him. She'd meant to sit down with Macon and force him to talk to her. Then she'd actually seen him. When she'd knocked on the back door, he'd opened it. He'd wiped his hands on his apron and given her the sweetest smile she'd ever seen, and when he'd asked what she needed her brain and her mouth hadn't worked at all in sync. She'd stumbled and told him she was looking for a job, and she'd started waiting tables that night.

How would he feel if he knew she had an ulterior motive? She promised herself every single night that she was going to tell him the truth, and every night she put it off. Now she was in too deep. She was caught in a trap of her own making.

"I can't. I'm closing." It was a perfect excuse and one she liked using. She took all the extra shifts she could. Besides needing the money, she liked the quiet after the restaurant was closed. She enjoyed the way Sean turned on music and everything seemed to slow down. They would sit and have a late dinner. Sometimes Sean's wife Grace would join them and she could watch how much they loved each other. If Grace brought their daughter, she could play with the baby.

"You're always closing." Deena frowned her way. "Some day you'll have to join us and have some fun."

"Of course." She handed Deena the eraser for the features board. "One day I won't be the new girl."

She put the working-late excuse on being the new girl. She couldn't explain that she didn't have enough cash for a deposit on an apartment and wouldn't for a while. She still had to make payments on her mother's hospital bills. Her mom had been so proud. She couldn't let it go, couldn't let her sink into bankruptcy even though she was gone.

Deena sighed. "Can you take the trash out? The bathrooms are clean, but the lobby trash is full. I swear Javier cleans out that truck of his with that can. I've told him twenty times to take it out back."

She nodded and walked to the front of the house. The entry trash was only about half full, but it was best to start with a clean slate. She quickly pulled the bag. There were several more beneath, always ready for a quick change. She fixed the new bag and closed the old.

"Thank you, darlin'!" Deena winked her way. "You're the best. I'm going to give you all the high rollers tonight."

Ally grinned and walked toward the back. She moved through the kitchen, enjoying the smells of the prep and the hum of activity.

She'd worked a few jobs before. Before her mom had gotten sick, she'd worked in the local fast food place. That had been pretty nasty, though she'd enjoyed the camaraderie. She'd worked two jobs after high school, saving every dime she'd made for four years. After Ronnie had gone into the service, she'd felt odd about leaving their mom alone for too long. She'd changed over to working part time for the church.

She pushed out of the back door and took a deep breath. Where had all those years gone? Why couldn't her mother have passed on before she knew Ronnie was gone? It seemed kinder. But the universe hadn't shown a hell of a lot of kindness to Ally's family.

With a heavy heart, she opened the bin and dumped the trash in. It would be dark soon and time for dinner service. For a few hours she could lose herself in work and not think about all the problems she needed to solve.

Macon Miles wasn't who she'd thought he was. Somehow she'd made him a monster in her mind, the one who survived when it should have been Ronnie. He'd taken her brother's place. She knew in her rational mind that wasn't fair, but it was how she felt at the time.

Macon was a big bear of a man. He was also well educated and, if rumors were true, he came from a wealthy family. She'd met his brother. Adam Miles was elegant and well spoken. They were the types of men who married women with college degrees and fancy careers and social connections. Three strikes and she was out. He was exactly the type of man she should shy away from because he would never get serious about a girl like her.

So why did her eyes trail toward him constantly? What was it about those big, strong hands molding delicate treats that made her daydream about impossible things?

Macon wasn't her type. Not even close. She didn't really have a type now that she thought about it. She'd only dated a couple of guys seriously and they were all willing to look past her shady family history. It wasn't easy to grow up in a small town where everyone knew about her father's crimes.

Ronnie hadn't cared. She could remember the first and only time she'd tried to run away after Carla Rowe had taken her in. Ronnie had run after her, still in his pajamas. He was a gangly kid. All arms and legs and big sad eyes. Everyone teased the hell out of him, but he'd sworn if she was leaving then he was, too. She was his sister, after all. He couldn't let her go alone, but he'd asked her to reconsider because the next night was mac and cheese night. He loved mac and cheese.

Another deep breath quelled the rising tide of emotion. She didn't need this. Ever since that day in the cemetery, it always seemed close to the surface, as though her subconscious knew that her other tasks were over and now it was time to deal with all that ugliness that lay beneath.

Well, it wasn't over. She had to stop dreaming about Macon Miles and find out the truth. If there was one thing she'd learned it was that even the sweetest of surfaces could hide something nasty. Soon she'd have enough money saved to hire the private investigator again and she would try to get the real reports, try to force them to tell the truth.

She was simply keeping an eye on Miles in the meantime. She wasn't falling for him. Nope. That would be stupid and she wasn't stupid.

She turned, ready to go back to work. Ally gasped as she came up against a hard chest.

"Hey, I was hoping to catch you alone." Timothy stared down at her. He was a good half a foot taller than she was. He didn't move back or give her any space at all.

She felt the hard metal of the trash bin at her back. God, she hated being crowded. "I need to get back to work."

His hand came up, blocking her from moving to her left. "I think they can spare you for a few minutes. I've been wanting to talk to you."

He was a perfectly made man with movie star good looks. Tim had fashionably cut blond hair. His face was quite lovely, but she'd always seen the hardness beneath his pretty exterior. He was a man who sneered instead of smiled, who only seemed to find humor at the expense of others. She'd heard him making fun of Macon when he stumbled one day, calling him a one-legged wonder.

Yeah, she didn't like Timothy. Her instincts told her to fight. She should push the asshole back and tell him she would rip his balls off if he touched her again.

But he was important here at Top. He was a European-trained chef and she was an easily replaceable waitress. She was well aware of how the world worked. If he wanted to, he could likely get her fired in a heartbeat. Sean would be sweet about it, but he couldn't take an unskilled laborer over a man who studied in France. From what she'd heard, he'd given Timothy a nice signing bonus when he'd agreed to work at Top. Sean was invested in this man. She had to be careful.

She inched to her right. "That's nice, but some other time. Deena needs me to help out with setup."

His other hand came down and she was trapped. "I think she's fine. She can certainly spare you for a few minutes. I've been watching you."

Yes, she was well aware. She'd been able to feel his lecherous stare like a spider crawling slowly across her skin. "I can't imagine why."

He moved in closer, until he was close enough for her to smell the liquor on his breath. God, she hated that smell. "I think you can."

Her stomach dropped. As much as she liked her job, she wasn't willing to let this idiot paw her over it. "Not really. I need to go back inside now."

He didn't move an inch. "I think you've been sending out signals."

Why did guys have to be jerks? "The only signals I've been sending out are for you to back off."

His lips curled up in that sneer he was always sporting. "So you want to play hard to get? I can understand that as long as you understand that the ending is going to be the same. I'm more than ready for you, sweetheart. Let me have a taste."

She was done. It was time to fight her way out. She brought her hands up, pushing against his chest. "Let me go."

He pushed back, proving how weak she was. "I will. Once I've got what I want."

Tears started to blur her vision. She hated this feeling. So weak and useless. Pathetic. "Let me go and I won't tell Chef what you tried."

He chuckled but it was a nasty sound. He pressed his body to hers. "You really think Taggart is going to listen to some two-bit whore over me? You're a dime a dozen. He can replace you in a heartbeat."

She hated that word. What she hated even more was the way some men used their strength against women, as though being bigger gave them rights. She brought her knee up as hard as she could, but she was too close. She caught his thigh and it only seemed to make him madder.

His right hand tangled in her hair, pulling and making her scalp ache. Pain sizzled along her skin, making her grit her teeth. "You're

26

going to pay for that, bitch."

And then she could breathe again. Timothy was gone in a flash and she heard a strangled shout before her eyes could process what was happening in front of her. She fell back against the Dumpster, only barely managing to stay on her feet.

Macon was here. He'd pulled Timothy off of her, but it seemed he wasn't satisfied with breaking them apart. He punched Timothy squarely in the gut and the older man hit the concrete. "You want to pick on someone your own size, asshole? Or do you get your kicks off raping women?"

Her hands were shaking, her whole body aflame with shock. They weren't alone in the alley anymore. It seemed like the entire staff of Top had come out to witness her humiliation. Tears poured from her eyes. They would all know what kind of trouble she'd gotten into. They would probably side with the man.

"The bitch wanted it," Timothy managed to squawk, holding his gut. "She asked me to come out here for a quickie. I'm going to sue the fuck out of you, you one-legged freak."

"Did he really say that?" Eric grinned. He was standing next to one of the line cooks, a big guy named Drake.

Drake shook his head. "I think so. Go on, Macon. Beat the little shit to death with your prosthetic."

"He doesn't need two legs to kill you, asshole," Eric said. "He could do it with no legs and one hand tied behind his back. I suggest you shut your trap."

They weren't reacting like she'd expected. There were no pitying looks her way. Eric gave her a reassuring smile.

"Let Macon handle it," Drake said, nodding her way. "The big guy can take care of this. Don't you worry."

Macon ignored everyone, choosing to put himself between her and Timothy. He didn't crowd her, didn't back her into a corner, simply offered himself as a wall against the man who'd tried to hurt her. "You okay?"

"Yes," was all she could manage.

"All right, let's break this up. We've got service in less than two hours." When Sean Taggart barked an order, every man snapped to attention. She'd heard rumors that Taggart had been a Green Beret. She believed them. The blond god of a man stalked out of the back door, gesturing for everyone to head back inside. He was six foot three, a bit shorter than Macon, but there was no question who was in charge. Chef Taggart had led men into battle.

He was also probably about to fire her.

Damn, but she'd liked this job. It wasn't fair.

When everyone was gone, he looked down at his pastry chef. Sean stepped up and reached down, giving Timothy a hand up. "Are you all right?"

At least the crowd was gone. There would only be a couple of people to watch her get fired.

Timothy's eyes narrowed as he allowed Sean to help him up. "No, I'm not all right and I have to insist that you fire that asshole. I was taking the girl up on her offer when that meathead came out and went berserk. I want the police out here. I'm having him arrested for assault."

Oh, god, she was going to get Macon arrested. She couldn't stand that thought. He'd tried to help her. "It wasn't Macon's fault."

Sean turned her way, one brow arched. "Really? Macon didn't rearrange this guy's intestines?"

She shook her head. She had to cover for him. "I did."

Macon stepped in front of her again, as though protecting her from both men now. "That's utterly ridiculous. It was me, boss. He was..."

Sean held a hand up. "Don't. I don't need an explanation."

"The cops will," Timothy said.

"Yes, and if you call them, I'm going to give them one," Taggart said before turning around and kicking Timothy squarely in the balls. Timothy groaned and fell back to the ground. Taggart turned back to her. "That is how you kick a guy in the balls, sweetheart. You gotta have a little space between the two of you and then you have to visualize your foot actually going into his body cavity. That way you put some power behind it. Don't forget that for next time. Miles, you all right?"

"I'd feel better if he was dead," Macon admitted.

Taggart gave him a sure smile. "He'll wish he was tomorrow."

"He's going to call the cops." Ally was still shaky. Sometimes cops didn't believe victims.

Taggart winked her way and pointed to a security camera placed above the back door. "He can and then he can explain why he was trying to rape an obviously unwilling woman. But he's not going to call anyone because if he does, I'm going to let Miles here take out his frustrations on him." Taggart took a knee beside the moaning Timothy. "Because if he tries to call the cops, I'll show him what we do to assholes who attempt to molest one of my female employees. Here's a hint. It's not pretty. We'll give him a Taggart special. My big brother has been dying to murder someone ever since his club blew up. Miles, take her inside and finish up your prep. I'm going to have an exit interview with this guy. Can you handle a promotion?"

Macon stilled, as though processing his good fortune. He nodded slowly, but there was a satisfied gleam in his eyes. "I can do it."

"Good because that's the last time I hire some dude from France." His eyes trailed to her. "Can you handle her? She's shaky."

"Yes, Chef. I'll take care of her." Macon reached out a hand.

She wasn't getting fired? She wasn't getting fired. The knowledge seeped into her like a warm blanket. She really should have tried harder. She would have liked to have been the reason Timothy had turned that peculiar shade of purple.

She looked at that big hand of Macon's. It was callused and rough and it had defended her. Maybe he'd been born with a silver spoon in his mouth, but it seemed like years in the Army and hard work in the civilian world had toughened him up. He wasn't the guy she'd thought he was.

"You don't have to be scared of me, sweetheart," he said quietly. "Let's go and I'll get you a drink and you can settle down. He's not going to hurt you. No one's going to hurt you here. Not while I'm around."

She put her hand in his and the minute that massive slab of flesh closed over hers, she felt warmer, stronger than before. Safer.

She followed him inside, her fingers tangling with his.

CHAPTER TWO

"That wind is picking up," Sean said as he stepped out into the alley. "Has anyone checked the weather?"

Macon hadn't worked at another restaurant, but he was fairly certain most head chefs didn't take out the trash. Sean dumped the bag and let the lid close with a crash.

"We're under a watch until two a.m. Both tornado and flashfloods." It wasn't raining yet, but there was a heaviness to the air he didn't like. Dinner service was long over and the rest of the staff had done their jobs. It was just him and Taggart and Ally.

"Okay, let's clean up and then I'll come in and do the books tomorrow. I don't want to risk getting cut off. The road into our neighborhood floods sometimes and I don't want Grace and Carys alone if we've got tornados to worry about."

"I'll do it." It seemed a shame to make the man come in on his day off when Macon didn't mind. "I wasn't doing anything else tonight anyway."

Except maybe talking to Ally. Since that moment he'd opened the door and realized she was in trouble, something had taken root in his chest. She needed someone to look out for her. She'd made a single, pitiful attempt to protect herself, but he hadn't missed how her eyes had slid away after he'd clocked Timothy the Ass. She'd expected to get fired. She'd been surprised when it didn't work out that way. She would have walked out with her head hung low if Taggart hadn't proven to be the man he was.

"Are you sure?" Taggart asked. "Because I was really looking forward to the day off. My stepsons are in town and I'd like to spend some time with them. I would owe you, man."

He shrugged. "If it gets really bad, I'll sleep on the sofa in your office. I've slept worse places. And besides, you don't owe me a thing. I appreciate how you handled Asswipe today."

Arms crossed over his big chest. "Yes, about that…I was planning on talking to you. Now seems as good a time as any. That girl is in trouble."

Well, Eric had warned him. He'd already made his decision. He'd made it the minute she'd put her trembling hand in his and laced their fingers together. He was an idiot but somehow she'd become his in that moment. "I'll take care of her."

Taggart's eyes narrowed and Macon was reminded of a dad looking out for his daughter. Taggart gave a damn about his employees. "Really? How much care are we talking about?"

"I don't know. I'm not declaring my love for her or anything. I barely know her. I'm attracted to her. It's not simply physical. I like her. She's a sweet kid."

"She's twenty-six. She's not a kid. And she's got some issues. I think she thought I was going to blame her for the incident."

Macon nodded. "Yeah, I caught that, too."

"Look, I've talked to Adam. I know you're not completely settled in. If you want, I'll find a way to take her home with me. She can stay in our guest room."

What was left unsaid was the fact that she wouldn't stay there for long. He'd been training at Sanctum for a few months now and even he recognized that Ally would likely enjoy D/s. It was all there in the way she deferred to those around her, the way her eyes slid away the minute someone she admired put some bite in his or her tone. As a long-term Dom, Sean wouldn't have missed any of that. Sean would introduce her to friends who would pick up on the highly submissive streak she had and before Ally knew it, she would be some well-meaning Dom's sub, taken care of and protected.

Fuck that.

"I said I'll take care of her."

31

Sean's lips curled up and he chuckled. "Damn, that's quite a look on your face. Okay. You'll take care of her. Let me know if you need anything. And service went well tonight. You did a great job."

All his doubt came back, needling him. "I don't have the education Timothy had."

Taggart shook his head. "You've got the skill. Practice a lot. Send anything you work on over to my brother's house. Ever since the twins were born my brother drowns himself in sweets. Seriously, he's getting fat. Fatherhood is putting a nice spare tire on the old boy. Big Tag is going to mean something totally different soon."

Were they talking about the same Ian Taggart? There wasn't an ounce of fat on that man. He was all muscle and sarcasm from what Macon could tell. Ian was his brother's favorite sparring partner. They could trade jibes all day long.

"Will do. I'm really thankful for the opportunity, Chef."

Sean put a hand on his arm. "Make the most of it. If you think you're in over your head, let me know. I'll be honest, I would rather go with you than find someone else. You're family. So we'll cook what you know for a couple of weeks. Practice at home and we'll expand the menu. We've got strawberries coming in Thursday. A big case of them. I'll expect something good."

His mom had a great recipe for strawberry pie and shortcake. He could tweak it, elevate it. He could make a shortbread cookie and whip his own cream with an infusion of vanilla that would truly show off the flavor of the berries.

"And you're off in your own world already figuring out how to use those berries. I told you, you'll be fine. You were born to do this job." Sean headed for the door. "And thanks for filling in on the paperwork. I can't tell you how much I appreciate it. There are pillows and blankets in the closet in my office. There's also a bottle of excellent Scotch you can dip into. And don't mind the other things you might see in there. They're only for play."

Dear god, that could mean anything coming from Sean or his friends. Macon had accidently walked in on Jake and Serena testing some sort of suspension thing Serena assured him was all for research. He'd seen way more of his sister-in-law than he'd ever expected to see and way, way more of his...well, of Jake.

He knocked now. He knocked a lot.

A raindrop fell, hitting him squarely in the forehead. It looked like one of those nights, but at least he wouldn't toss and turn. Doing the books would give him something to do. He stepped back into the kitchen and walked toward the front of house.

He would get right on that paperwork after he dealt with the problem of Ally Jones.

He strode through the door that separated the kitchen from the dining area as Sean was waving good-bye to Ally. Chef Taggart ducked out into the rain.

And they were alone.

"Sean said you're working on the books so he could head home before the storm." She glanced at the doors Sean had gone through.

He needed to lock those suckers. He made quick work of it and pulled the blinds closed.

When he turned back around, she was clutching the broom she held like it was a lifeline. Maybe this wouldn't be so easy. "Do you want to hold the keys?" He placed them on the hostess desk and backed away. "That way you know you can leave when you want to."

She sighed. "God, am I that much of a scared mouse?"

He wouldn't put it that harshly. "It's obvious you don't trust men."

"It's not like that. I'm jittery from earlier. I'm sorry. It's nothing personal."

"I won't take it personally, Ally. We've all got scars. Some of us wear them on the outside and some of us got 'em buried deep. You don't feel comfortable being alone with me, but I promise you have nothing to worry about. How can I make you feel better? You got a phone on you? You can keep it close. There's an emergency button on most phones. You can call it without having to unlock the phone."

Her eyes rolled. "Fine. You're not the big bad wolf." She walked up to him, putting her feet in front of his. She had to turn her neck up to see him. "I'm not scared of you. You're a big old teddy bear, but you're not like a lot of the men I grew up around. They were a bit more like Timothy."

He had the most insane urge to reach out and tangle his hands in that soft brown hair of hers. It was in a bun on the back of her head, but he'd seen it long, flowing down her back. When the sunlight hit her hair he could see strands of brown and red and yellow. Complex. Like the woman herself. Like a lemon tart. Sweet and sour and perfect. "Is that why you thought Sean was going to believe Timothy?"

She took a step back and started sweeping the lobby. "It wouldn't be the first time someone believed a male employee over a female one."

So it had happened to her before. "I wouldn't have believed it. Even if he'd had his tongue halfway down your throat I would have thought he was assaulting you."

She stopped and looked at him thoughtfully. "Because you think I'm too sweet to have an affair with a coworker?"

"You're too sweet to want that asshat." Damn, he probably shouldn't have said that. He could feel himself blushing. "I'm sorry. That was inappropriate."

She sighed. "It wasn't. I said it first. And I'm sorry if I made you think I'm some fainting female. I'm not. I can take care of myself. Usually. I'm afraid that asshat brought back a whole ton of bad memories. When I was fifteen I worked at a movie theater and the manager there was a big fan of inappropriate touching. When I complained, I found myself out of a job. He was the owner's son. It's not the only crappy thing in my background. Most women have a file marked 'skeevy dudes' in their personal histories. I'm sorry. I had a bad reaction."

"You should have a bad reaction. You weren't yelling."

She frowned. "It's embarrassing."

"Why? If some dude was trying to mack down on me and I didn't like it, I wouldn't be embarrassed. I'd be pissed." He needed to figure out what was going on in her head. "No one thought less of you, Ally. Did you think they would?"

"Maybe."

He crossed the distance between them. She was turned away. He didn't try to hide his steps. He wanted her to know he was behind her. He put his hands on her shoulders. "What happened today was on him. Not you. Him. The next time some idiot so much as touches you, you scream and shout for help and one of us will come running."

"Like you're touching me now?"

He pulled his hands back. "Sorry."

She turned and he was happy to see a smile on her face. "Now I know how to get to you, Miles. You're a sucker for a down-on-her-luck girl."

Was she flirting with him? "I'm a down-on-my-luck guy. I guess like attracts like."

She studied him for a moment and he wished he'd shaved. He was a little scruffy. He really wasn't kidding about being down on his luck. "Why did you show up today? You weren't taking out the trash and you don't smoke."

He thought about lying and then decided not to go that way. "I was looking for you."

"Why?"

"I wanted to talk to you. I heard a rumor."

Her jaw went tight. "Really?"

He didn't like the militant light in her eyes, but he plowed ahead anyway. "Yeah, are you living in your car?"

She waved that off with a laugh. "Oh, that. Yes. I can't afford a place close to work yet. I'll find something in a couple of weeks."

He didn't understand her. She was acting like homelessness was a nothing problem she would deal with later. "It's dangerous."

"No more so than anywhere else. I wasn't exactly safe here at work earlier. At least I can lock the doors. And the horn makes a really good deterrent. Not to mention my LifeHammer. Sounds silly. It's really supposed to be for breaking a window if your car goes underwater. Not surprisingly, it also works on car thieves and pushy drug dealers."

She was going to give him a heart attack. "You took a hammer to a guy trying to jack your car?"

One shoulder shrugged and she went back to sweeping. "Yeah. After I brought that sucker down on his hand, he decided to try again elsewhere. And the drug dealer was actually kind of nice. I mean in the beginning. He was just getting started and his sales pitch needed work. Then he tried to rob me and he met my life hammer, too."

He opened his mouth but nothing came out. What was he supposed to say to that?

She kept on. "I would have called the cops, but I don't exactly have a cell. It's sweet of you to tell me how to protect myself. Oddly, most guys who intend to harm me don't give me lectures on protecting myself."

The rain was starting to come down hard, beating against the rooftop. He finally managed to find some proper words. "You can't stay in your car."

"Sure I can."

His first instinct was to tell her what she was going to do, but he had to wonder if she would come after him with that hammer. The woman in front of him was a far cry from the one who hadn't screamed out when Timothy cornered her. He was smart enough to understand. She was comfortable with him. She could joke because she didn't believe he would hurt her. If he applied some pressure, intimidated her, he would likely get her to do what he wanted. And that would make him one more asshole who used her. "It makes me nervous. Especially on a night like this. Maybe you could stay in Sean's office tonight?"

He would sleep on the floor. He hadn't been joking. He'd slept in much worse places. Hell, no one was shooting at him. He called it a win.

"You think you should drive home in this mess?" She peeked out through the blinds.

"I don't have a car. I take the train. Station's right down the street." He would rather stay with her, but now that he thought about it, she might be uncomfortable with that. If he was leaving, he would have to be fast though. DART didn't run all night. He could call Adam, but he felt like an idiot calling his big brother to pick him up from work. He was thirty years old. He'd been driving since he was sixteen.

He couldn't work the gas pedal anymore and getting a vehicle fitted for him would cost more money than he had.

She perked up. "I have a car. I can totally give you a ride. And the good news is if we find ourselves in high water, I can also smash through the windshield."

"You are entirely too invested in that hammer."

She chuckled. "Maybe. I'm really okay, Miles. Despite the idiocy of this afternoon, I've been taking care of myself for a long time. It's not the first time I've been on my own. Hell, I have a car. It's practically the Ritz compared to some of the places I've slept."

"You've been homeless before?" He'd had a rough childhood. Not financially. He'd had all the money he needed, but he'd been raised in military academies, and they weren't the best at giving a child affection. Talking to Kai for all these weeks had taught him that affection was something he needed. But he couldn't imagine being a homeless kid.

"Sure. I was once given a blue ribbon by this cop in my hometown. He said I was the best runaway he'd ever seen. I might have said I couldn't be too good since he kept catching me, but he told me he liked to reward persistence."

"What were you running away from?" He asked the question, but had an idea. She could go up against drug dealers and car thieves, but she turned into a mouse around an authority figure trying to take advantage of her.

"My dad was kind of a jerk." She finished sweeping up and turned to him. "Did I say thank you for saving me today? I don't usually play the damsel in distress but you were a damn fine knight."

"There's no shining armor here, sweetheart." He'd given that up long ago. Actually, when he really thought about it, he'd never been the type.

"Let's see. You served your country honorably, you help out your boss, save waitresses from nasty assholes. You're looking pretty shiny to me, Miles."

She set the broom aside and something shifted in the room. He could see it in the way she relaxed as she moved toward him.

What was she doing? The air suddenly seemed more sultry than before. "I'm no hero. I went in the Army because it was expected of me."

"That's what a hero usually says. Why were you really looking for me, Miles?" She stepped up, leaving very little space between them.

"I told you."

"Yes, you wanted to find out about my living situation. Do you treat all the waitresses like this?"

"No." He tended to leave them alone. They were attractive women, but he didn't have anything to offer a girlfriend. He could barely take care of himself. He knew he should stay away from her, too, but she moved him in a way he hadn't felt before.

"So why me?"

"I like you." Yep he sounded like a junior high kid.

"I like you, too. I didn't think I would, but I can't deny it." She went up on her toes and her hands were suddenly flat against his chest. "This is a mistake. It's a horrible mistake, and I hope you're smart enough to stop me."

She was straining, lifting herself up as tall as she could go.

"I'm not that smart, sweetheart." He lowered his head and let his lips touch hers.

His whole body went on alert. His cock tightened immediately and his body felt like it locked around hers. All he could see or smell or taste

37

was Ally. She became the freaking center of his universe and all he'd done was brush his lips against hers.

He was in too deep, but there was no way he was backing away now.

* * * *

It was wrong. She knew it the minute she got close to him. Hell, she knew it the minute Chef Taggart had walked out the door, leaving her alone with the single sexiest man she'd ever laid eyes on. Macon made her heart pound, but he was also the one man in the world she shouldn't touch since she was lying to him.

The instant she'd seen him, she'd changed all her plans. It was wrong, but it was also true.

Kiss him. Kiss him once and you'll find out it isn't as good as you think it will be. Sex isn't really all that special. It's not like you haven't tried it before. It's kind of messy and then it's over. It would probably be the same with this guy.

Or it will be so much better because this is a man and not a boy and damn, but he looks like he could take care of business, if you know what I mean.

Her inner voice had a split personality and an overabundance of sauciness it seemed. Still, she was kind of going with optimism as Macon's gorgeous face dropped down.

His lips were soft as they brushed against hers. He didn't overwhelm her the way some men had tried before. He went slow, as though enjoying exploring her. His hands moved from her shoulders to her back, running the length of her spine and making her shiver. Her chest bumped against his. She could feel the way her nipples pebbled, and her whole body seemed to go soft.

All her previous sexual experience had been about obliterating something. Whether it be herself or some bad day or horrifically bad news. It had been about escaping.

She didn't want to escape this.

She breathed him in. He smelled liked lemons and mangoes and an underlying hint of sweetness. His hands were so big and callused, but they moved gently against her skin.

And then it was gone.

38

"Did you hear that?" He looked toward the doors.

She'd heard the pounding of her heart. She'd kind of ignored everything else.

In the distance, she could hear the sound of a siren going off. "I think that's the warning system. Don't panic. They cover a lot of space. We need to find an interior room and wait it out. The bathroom is best. There aren't any windows there."

"I'm going to go grab the radio. There's a hand crank radio we keep in the kitchen. It's also a flashlight and we might need that. It's a good sign that the lights aren't out."

She nodded. "Yes. I'll go with you."

He put two hands on her arms. "No. Go get in the bathroom. Get your head down. I'll be there in a minute."

He disappeared into the kitchen. She stood there, listening to the sound of the rain beating on the roof. He was right. They would need the radio so they would know when all was clear. At least it was late. No one would be on the streets at this time of night. Damn Mother Nature. She had terrible timing.

The phone at the hostess station rang. Despite the fact that it was so late, she decided to answer rather than let it go to voicemail. It could be Sean having car trouble. "This is Top."

The voice came over the line in fits and starts. Deena. "… okay?... heard… coming… Top."

"What?" She strained to hear her. Deena would be calling from her cell. It looked like the weather was hurting her signal.

"Worried…"

The line went dead and so did the lights. They didn't even flicker. There was a loud popping sound and then everything went dark.

She stood still for a moment, trying to orient herself. They'd drawn the shades so only the barest hint of what light was left outside filtered in. She was utterly in the dark. Her heart was pounding for a different reason now. Fear sparked through her. Her instinct was to burrow down in the bathroom. It was back and to her left. All she had to do was walk about three feet in a straight line and she would find the back wall. Once she could touch it, she would follow it back to the bathrooms. Simple. She would be safe there.

There was a loud crash and then it sounded like the world was being battered.

The windows. At least one of them had shattered. Her eyes were adjusting and she could see a couple of big balls that had gotten through the shades. They looked like baseballs, but she knew what they were. Hail. She heard another crash, this one to her right. The kitchen.

She didn't think, simply reacted. She ran to her right. Something was wrong. Macon knew exactly where the radio and flashlights were. He should have been back here. He wouldn't have left her alone. She'd known him for a few weeks and he was a man who tried to take care of the people around him. She'd found it annoying at first. She'd had to let him walk her to her car at night, which meant trying to hide the fact that she was living in it. At first she'd enjoyed the nights Macon had off, but she'd quickly come to appreciate the feeling of being watched over by him. Sure, he did it for all the women, but she'd pretended it was only for her.

She hit the double doors to the kitchen at a jog. She could sort of see.

Something crunched underneath her. More glass. The back window had gone.

"Macon?" Nothing. "Macon!"

Lightning flashed and she saw him. He was on the floor, the flashlight next to him. Her hands started to shake as she made her way to him. Something dark was on his face. Please don't let it be blood. Please don't let it be. He was so close to the prep station. It looked like he'd slipped and hit his head.

The world suddenly went eerily quiet.

Even as she hit her knees, she knew things hadn't gotten better. They'd gotten infinitely more dangerous. Quiet was bad. Quiet meant the monster had found her.

"Macon? Please get up. We have to go. It's almost here." Panic threatened. She reached for his hand. It was warm in hers and when she tried to find his pulse, it was strong under her fingertip. His heart was beating.

The street kid inside her told her to run, to hide, to protect herself. She'd spent those first years of her life in survival mode. She'd not known anything else until she'd been taken in by her mom and Ronnie. It would be easy to slip back into it. Hell, she'd been in it since her mother died. The child she'd been had taken over and she looked out for herself. That child urged her to take the radio and the flashlight and hide. No one would blame her.

But she wasn't a child any longer. She'd indulged that piece of herself for too long. She couldn't leave him. She stood up and grasped his hands in hers. Maybe she could make it to the storage closet. It was reinforced. It might be their best bet. She took a deep breath and started to pull him.

Tried to pull him and didn't get far.

"You had to be all muscular, didn't you?" She tried again, but he wouldn't move.

There was a terrible sound that filled her whole world. If she hadn't known better, she would have thought a train was coming her way. It wasn't a train. Tears filled her eyes and panic made her want to flee, but she dropped back down and did the only thing she could.

CHAPTER THREE

"And they're sure his hands are going to work? It's just his brain that was bashed in? Wait, he needs his brain to cook, right? I know you don't but what he does is so much more important." A deep voice disturbed Macon's sleep.

"Have I ever told you what an asshole you are?" Another voice. This one was very familiar, but Macon kind of wanted all of the voices to go away.

They seemed intent on tormenting him. "Maybe a couple of times, but this is serious, Sean. He's an artist. If he dies, the world loses. Why couldn't I have met him when I was in the Army instead of his brother? Adam is utterly useless unless you need someone to make sarcastic comments at inopportune times."

"Yeah, and we all know that's your job."

His head ached. What the hell had happened? He didn't remember dipping into the whiskey. He hadn't done that for a while. He had work so he couldn't drink all night and moan the loss of his leg. Not when there were pies to prep. Why had he started in again?

"Fuck you, Big Tag. And the next time you piss off some fifth grade hacker and your e-mail gets inundated with ads for erectile dysfunction and tractors, you're on your own." His brother was here? Why was his brother present at his hangover?

"That was Chelsea. She gets pissy from time to time."

"Oh, and my sarcasm is so much smarter than your sarcasm," his brother announced.

"Could your sarcasm be a little quieter?" He managed to get his eyes to open up. He closed them immediately. The world was way too bright. He started to stretch and found himself tethered to an IV. Shit. He was in the hospital. How many damn times was he going to wake up in a hospital?

He reached down and touched his good leg.

Adam leaned over. "It's still there. You're good. You're at Parkland Hospital in Dallas."

It was stupid but he was deeply grateful to his brother in that moment. Adam didn't make fun of him for worrying. He simply explained.

"I'll get Daley," a deep voice said. He was fairly certain he was dealing with both Taggarts, plus Adam. And he'd gotten a glimpse of something pink. Had Ian Taggart been wearing a pink shirt?

"Hey, brother. Way to survive a tornado." Adam's hand clasped his forearm. "I've been here for years and never actually seen one of the fuckers. You're here for a few months and get caught in one. You are one unlucky son of a bitch."

Yep. That was him. He groaned as he tried to open his eyes again. The last year had been one gut punch after another. IED and then fighting off insurgents with one leg. Watching Ronnie…no. He wasn't going there. It was so much easier to think about how his ex-wife had screwed him over and taken everything.

The only good thing to happen to him in that last year was…

He forced his eyes open. "Ally? Ally was with me." He gripped his brother's arm. "Ally was in the bathroom."

Sean Taggart shook his head. "No, she wasn't."

"Oh, god, what happened?" Ally couldn't be dead. He'd told her where to go, how to protect herself. Memories came flooding back. He'd grabbed the flashlight right before the lights went out. And then everything had gone dark and he tripped over something with his stupid non-leg and he'd fallen. He'd bashed his head and right before he'd gone out he'd been happy that Ally was safe.

Ally hadn't been safe?

His boss looked across the bed to grin at his brother. "Told you." He glanced down toward Macon. "Ally disobeyed and you're lucky she's a brat. They found her covering your body with hers. She protected your head with her back and it was a good thing. When the tornado hit all the pots we had hanging overhead fell and they would have come right down on your noggin."

"Or your hands." Ian Taggart strode back into the room. There was a pink blanket wrapped over his massive chest. It was a weird fashion statement for a former Green Beret to make. "They could have crushed your hands. She's a goddamn hero."

Big Tag was fond of his lemon pie.

Ally had done what? His brain wasn't quite functioning. He had to process the information. "Who found us? Where is Ally?"

"The crew was at a bar in Deep Ellum," Sean explained. "When they heard where the tornado hit, they came running. They found you in the kitchen with Ally protecting your nasty ass."

"She's alive?"

Sean moved to his left and gestured toward the window. "She's fine. She's asleep. I convinced the nurses to bring in a cot and let her spend the night."

He sat up despite the knife that threatened to split his brain in two. She was lying across a small cot, her body curled up and her back to the wall. Her arms were crossed over her chest and there was something about the way she slept that made him think she was protecting herself.

"She covered my body with hers?" He let his voice go low, not wanting to disturb her.

"Yeah and she's got the bruises to prove it," Sean said. "Her back took a couple of nice whacks, but would you like to know what she said when we tried to get her into the ER?"

"She wouldn't go because she can't afford it." He knew what Ally's first fear would be. She wouldn't want to run up a bunch of bills she couldn't afford. "She hasn't been around long enough. Her insurance hasn't kicked in."

"Yep. I brought in a friend of mine. He checked her out. She's fine. And she can sleep through anything," Ian said as his pink blanket moved. The big guy looked down. "Root around all you like, baby girl. Nothing's coming out of that. I need to take her to her momma. Kenzie should be finished by now. The girl eats like a Hoover. She makes Daddy proud."

"Charlotte's here?"

"Of course. Dude, you're important to us. You make the pies."

"What Ian is trying to say is you're family," Adam said, rolling his eyes. "Everyone's out in the waiting room. Charlotte and Avery are having a breast in. Some dude was dumb enough to tell them to find somewhere private to feed the babies, so now they're letting it all hang out in protest."

The door opened and a tall man in a white coat walked in. "Good morning, Adam's brother. I'm Will Daley. I'll be making sure your brain is functioning today."

"Ask him if he remembers how to make the pies, doc," Ian said before heading off to find his wife.

"Sorry about my brother. He's an idiot," Sean said as Will took a look at his chart.

"He's also more sarcastic than usual when he's freaked out. He thought Sean was closing," Adam explained. "He showed up a few minutes after the crew. He was the one who forced everyone to wait for the ambulance. Ally was going to try to get you into her car to take you to the hospital."

"Ian acts like an ass most of the time, but he really does have a heart of gold," Sean said. "I think you'll discover my brother believes he owes you for more than good pies. And so do I."

"Is she really all right?" He couldn't take his eyes off Ally.

"That one is stubborn as hell, but she seems fine," the doctor said.

"You checked her out?" When Ian said he'd brought a friend in, Macon thought it was likely an old Army buddy with some medic training. He would feel so much better if a practicing doctor had examined her.

Will pulled out a penlight. "Yes, I did. I had to promise there would be no paperwork. That girl is terrified of hospital bills. Not that I blame her. Yours is going to be a doozy. Let me take a look at your eyes."

After a few moments of flashing too-bright lights in his eyes, Will proclaimed him ready to go home. He'd taken a whack to his head, but Will hadn't seen any real damage in the incredibly expensive CT scan he'd been put through. "I can release you today, but I want you to rest for a few days. With your leg injury, you could be off balance. You're not long post op, are you?"

He shook his head, uncomfortable even talking about it. He knew Ally knew, but he'd been careful around her. She hadn't seen him trip or have to adjust the damn thing. She certainly hadn't seen his stump. Knowing and seeing were two different things. "It's been almost a year."

"Well, it can take even longer for you to get truly confortable with the prosthetic. I noticed your organic leg is banged up."

"What?" Adam asked.

His brother could be a mother hen at times. "I fell while I was jogging."

Will held up a hand, stopping Adam's next comment. "It's good. You should attempt to do all the things you did before. Trying to get back to normal is an excellent sign, but you have to take better care of those scrapes and lay off the running for a week. You need someone to keep an eye on you for the next few days and I'll need to see you again in about a week."

"We'll take care of it, Will," Adam said.

"No. I will."

Everyone turned to look at the woman who had said the words. Ally sat up, blinking and then covering her yawn. She looked like a sleepy kitten waking up. She stood up and stretched, her breasts moving against the thin fabric of her T-shirt.

"He's not the only one who needs watching after," Daley said with a frown, looking her way. "I have no idea how you slept on that thing. Aren't you sore?"

She shook her head. "I've had worse. Look, Miles and I can watch out for each other. You've got a place, right?"

Despite the events of the night before, she looked pretty and young. He probably looked really rough. "Yeah, but it's really my brother's guesthouse."

She shrugged. "Digs is digs, Miles. You've got a place to crash and I have a car. Yeah, the restaurant might not have survived but Bessie did. And to think all those stupid mechanics wanted to put her down when she hit two hundred K. So between the two of us, we are practically a fully functional human being."

"With three and a quarter legs." The sarcasm was catching.

"Yep. We got those, too. And stop complaining. You've got a three-quarters bionic leg. What do you say, Miles? Can I crash at your place for a while and we can get the docs off our backs?"

He nodded and then winced. Damn, they were a sad couple.

Couple. He'd kissed her. It had been going somewhere until Mother

Nature decided to try to kill them.

She slapped her hands together. "Cool. Then lay it on me, Doc. What do I need to watch for with the big guy?"

She and Will stepped outside, talking about pain medications and side effects.

"Is the restaurant gone?" They might have less than Ally said. They might be down two jobs.

Sean shook his head. "She's exaggerating. We've got blown windows and some minor damage. We'll be open again in a week, which will give you plenty of time to recover. I'm going to find someone else to do the desserts for the parties. You need to rest."

Sean was hosting a birthday party for his wife this weekend. Two actually. There was a family party on Saturday afternoon and an adults-only party at Adam, Jake, and Serena's that night. Macon had already planned a spectacular cake. "Don't. I'll be fine in a couple of days. I want to do it."

"If you're sure, but if you change your mind give me a day or two," Sean said. "I'll go let the crew know they can come in and see you."

"Are there really a bunch of people waiting to see me?" Macon asked after the door closed.

Adam nodded. "Yeah, it's not like home, buddy. These people give a shit. There have been times that we're all we have so we stick together. Are you really feeling all right?"

"I feel like hell." He smiled. "And I feel great, too."

"Because of Ally?"

He shrugged. "She's cool."

Adam leaned over, his hands on the metal railing of the bed. "She was adamant about not being admitted, Macon. I got here right as the ambulance did and she was a little off."

"Well, she'd just survived a tornado." He felt off, too. And they were going to have a long talk about who was in charge when Taggart wasn't around. She hadn't obeyed his very reasonable commands.

Of course if she had, he might be dead, so maybe he'd rethink the lecture and make her some pancakes instead.

She'd also joked about his leg, so maybe she wasn't entirely adverse to it.

"It wasn't that and it wasn't only about the money. I tried to explain workman's comp to her. It would cover everything and I know damn well Sean is paid up, but she wouldn't listen," Adam explained. "She got really upset when they asked for ID."

"If they get her ID they can bill her." He thought he was starting to understand her. She'd been closed off, with all kinds of walls up, but he liked the woman who wasn't hiding from him. She was funny and maybe the tiniest bit insane. It was like she'd opened up to him after the day's incident with that asshat, Timothy. Or yesterday's. "How long was I out?"

"A night. It's almost noon. And I would bet a lot she wasn't as worried about the money as she was handing over that ID. She didn't want them to see it. I think she might be hiding something."

His brother could be paranoid. It came with the territory. He worked in high-level security, the kind that sometimes got co-opted by the CIA. Adam had gone from being a soldier to being what their father called a mercenary. Now that he'd seen Adam in action, he would simply call him a hero. But he was a paranoid hero.

"I don't think she's trying to hide anything except the fact that she's broke, and I have no room to complain there. It's not like I'm rolling in it." He stopped, coming up with another reason his brother might have a problem with Ally. "If you don't want her in the guesthouse, say so."

His brother's eyes narrowed. "And if I said so? What would you do?"

"Get an apartment," he replied.

"Shit, you want her."

"I like her." And he wanted her. She was the first woman he'd wanted in forever and that scared him because he hadn't exactly tried having sex since he'd lost his leg. He'd been afraid his dick didn't work anymore, but she'd fixed that problem. "I like her a lot."

"Yeah, you like her in a 'give up my nice house and go live somewhere scary because at least we're together' way." He sighed and shook his head. "Of course she's welcome. Sean says she's passed all his background checks, so we're good. Also, she saved you so her goodwill bank is full with me. She's hiding something and it's going to come out in the end. Do you want me to run a check on her?"

Sean would have run a cursory check, the same most employers did. Adam would delve into her background, peeling her apart like an onion and going through every layer. He would be ruthless about it and Macon was sure that once Adam was on the case, he would know everything there was to know about Allyson Jones. Including the stuff she might not want him to know.

"No. If I need to know she'll tell me."

"And if she decides you don't?"

"It's not a grand love affair, Adam. She needs a place to stay. I need someone to make sure my brain's not bleeding. I'm sure she'll be out and on her own in a week or two."

Adam huffed. "No way. That's one stray who's looking for a home. I've seen it. Sometimes they really like to drift, but not that one. She took the first responsibility she could. She sacrificed for you the minute it came up. She might not think she's looking for long term, but she'll get comfortable. You better be sure you like her because getting rid of her might be hard on both of you."

He wasn't going to sic Adam on her. She'd saved him. She'd risked her life for his and if she had some secret…well, who didn't? There were things he would never tell her. He would never give her the full story of what happened the day he lost his leg.

"Okay, I'll back off," Adam said. "Now, I'm going to let the hoard in. That is one mean-looking set of cooks, man. Do all restaurant employees look so rough?"

He grinned. "They do when they work at Top."

For the first time in a long time, he felt like he belonged somewhere. He sat back as Adam called the first visitors in.

* * * *

"I'd really feel better if you let me run a few tests." Will Daley was a handsome man. He was also stubborn.

"I'm fine." Her back hurt like a mother, but she wasn't about to run up thousands of dollars of debt when she could take some Advil and be good as new in a couple of days. Well, except she was fairly certain she'd developed a new fear of storms, but hey, what was one more phobia to add to the list?

"If you need me, call." He handed her his card.

"I will." She would for Macon.

The doctor shook his head and walked away.

"I think you frustrated the hot doc." Deena walked up carrying two coffees.

"Tell me you got some sleep." Deena was still wearing her cute top and blingy jeans from the night before.

She smiled, her lips curling up as she handed Ally the coffee. "I napped against Eric. He might look like all hard muscles, but he makes a nice pillow." She frowned suddenly. "Oh, god. What if I snored? I'm pretty sure I snore, and not in a sweet snuffle way. Do you think the fact that I sound like a dying elephant will turn him off?"

It had been so long since she'd had a friend like Deena. Maybe never. She'd been that trashy Jones kid back in her hometown, the one whose dad went to jail. No one here cared about how awful her father had been. No one knew how much trouble she was. "You don't sound like an elephant. It's really more like a rhino."

Deena slapped playfully at her arm and then gasped. "I'm so sorry."

Ally shook her head. "I'm fine. I'm bruised, that's all."

She'd had way worse. This was going to be an ache, but she kind of liked it. She'd earned this ache. She'd done good.

Deena's eyes filled with tears. "I can't believe you did that. You know they're saying he might have died without you."

She wasn't so sure of that. "I don't know. He's got a thick skull."

"Stop. You need to stop being so modest and start thinking properly. You know what Macon's reputation is, right?"

"He's a nice guy?" He'd always been nice to her. Was he nice to the other waitresses? Sure. Maybe he was really nice to them. She'd noticed Jenni and Tiffany in the waiting room. They were two of the other servers. Both were young and pretty and probably had never spent a night on the streets or attacked a drug dealer with a hammer. Jenni was a petite blonde working her way through college, while Tiffany was an artist of some kind. She had the willowy figure found on magazine covers.

Ally was kind of short, and since she'd started eating at Top, she'd filled way out. What if Macon kissed any woman who totally threw herself at him?

"Macon is known as the great deflector," Deena said as they walked toward the waiting room. "I gave him the nickname myself when I noticed how easily he deflected Jenni's every attempt to trap him. That poor girl had it so bad. I don't think it's because she's passionately in love with him. She's the kind of girl who notices when a guy doesn't notice and then she's all over him."

She knew the type. They annoyed her. "But everyone notices Jenni. The girl can't walk into the kitchen without someone telling her how good she looks."

"Because the other guys are smart," Deena explained. "She's a sweet kid, but none of these guys are interested in a kid. When Eric figured out her game, he hit on her once, let her turn him down, and now she leaves him alone. She's perfectly satisfied with getting some compliments, but Macon ignores her. She trapped him in the storage closet once and I swear I've never seen a dude run so fast. For a guy with a C-Leg, he's a gazelle when he wants to get away."

"So he's not a player." She liked that he didn't bother to play Jenni's game. Maybe she should have a talk with Jenni.

"Not at all. I thought he might play for the other team. Until you walked in."

"What does that mean?"

Deena took a sip of her coffee, her heels clacking on the laminate floors. "That man watches you like a hawk. I swear he practically drools when you bend over. He's got a thing for your backside."

She needed to stop doing that. She wasn't sure she wanted Macon watching her fat ass. "But my butt's really big."

"I believe the word he would use is juicy," Deena corrected. "Most men don't go for skinny things. That's a lie perpetuated by the media and skinny bitches. I dropped down to my ideal size and the sex dried up. The boys like me with about ten extra pounds."

"Macon stares at my ass?"

"Yep."

"I kissed him last night." That popped out of her mouth. She hadn't really meant to let anyone know about that. Restaurant life ran on gossip.

Deena stopped in the middle of the hall, her eyes wide. "When he was unconscious? Did you pull up the shirt? Because I bet he's hiding a six-pack. He never takes off his shirt. I've thought about spilling water on him so I can see his chest."

"Of course not when he was unconscious. Before he was unconscious." She couldn't really blame her friend. She wanted to see his chest, too. There was a basketball hoop in the back parking lot and sometimes the guys played before they opened. They would pick shirts or skins, but Macon always stayed back, simply watching. Maybe she was being silly, but she thought there was a sadness when he stood there.

The guys encouraged him to play, but he would shake his head.

Deena smiled. "And he kissed you back?"

He'd pulled her into the heat of his body and kissed her until she'd been breathless. "Yeah. I like him."

"And he obviously likes you, so why do I hear a 'but' coming up?"

"I know something he doesn't and when he finds out, he might not like me anymore."

Deena stopped. "What are you saying?"

What was she saying? Why had she even mentioned that? She'd been about to blurt out the truth concerning her past to Deena. She quickly recovered. There was more than one reason Macon might have issues with her. "I don't know. I heard he comes from a wealthy background and sometimes guys like that don't like the girl from the wrong side of the tracks."

She wasn't sure exactly what had happened with him. Ronnie had talked about Macon being from a wealthy family, how he always had money but he wasn't snooty.

Ronnie. She'd forgotten all about Ronnie the last few weeks. She'd gotten caught up in how gorgeous Macon Miles was and forgot that he was the only person alive who could tell her what happened to her brother.

And he refused to speak with her.

She'd even sent him an e-mail from one of the computers at the library. She'd sent it from the e-mail account she'd had back at home, one of the free kind. She'd asked him very politely if he would give her any information about Ronnie's death.

He hadn't replied.

What was she supposed to think of that? How did she reconcile the sweet, kind man she knew with the asshole who hadn't replied to a dying woman's pleas? She wasn't the only one Macon had refused to answer.

"Oh, Macon's not like that and from what I heard, he lost everything in the divorce."

She'd wondered what happened to his wife. Ronnie hadn't mentioned her. When she'd come to Top, she'd discovered that Macon had been married and had gone through a nasty divorce.

"Well, I'm sorry he lost everything because I like the man." She hoped he hadn't had anything to do with Ronnie's death or the cover-up. She prayed he didn't because she was pretty sure she was crazy about the man and it would break her heart. "I'm going to stay with him while he's recovering."

"You are?"

She nodded. "Yeah."

"Like with him, with him?"

That was the big question. That kiss last night had been spontaneous. Of course, waking up and hearing his low rumble and the doctor saying Macon needed someone to watch over him had spurred her to spontaneously offer to be his new roommate.

Why had she done that? Was it because getting closer to him might bring her the answers she was seeking? Or because she simply wanted to be closer to him?

"I'll stay in the guest room. I'm going to be there for him." They turned to walk into the waiting room.

"Wow, that's a lot of boobs," Deena said, her eyes wide.

"I think it's nice." There was nothing sexual about women feeding their babies.

"It's not right. They should cover up." An older man was complaining to the volunteer who sat at the desk.

"I've asked them to go to the bathroom, but they won't go," the woman whispered back as though she feared being overheard.

"Shit." Deena leaned over and whispered in her ear. "That's Charlotte Taggart, the big guy's wife. She recently had twins. And the other one is Avery O'Donnell. She's married to the big scary Irish guy in the back. This could get nasty."

Ally didn't understand why. The Avery lady's baby had his hand covering most of her breast as he suckled. Charlotte Taggart's very nice breast was bare for a second as she handed off one tiny bundle and accepted the other from her husband. The baby immediately went to work. It was sweet. She knew Big Tag from the restaurant. He was the one Macon made pies for. He tucked his baby daughter into the sling he was wearing. Even though the sling was the cutest pink it didn't make Big Tag any less masculine.

He looked over where the man was making a fuss. This could get ugly.

"Well ask them to leave," the man said, his face turning red. "My mother is having a procedure done. I shouldn't have to watch pornography."

Ian's eyes narrowed.

It was going to get really nasty.

The woman stood up and smoothed down her very sensible blouse. "I'll explain that they're being offensive."

"No, they're not," an elderly lady sitting near the door said. She pointed the cane she was holding at the complaining man. "They're taking care of their babies. He's a sad old codger who's never seen a breast before. If you don't like it, don't look."

"They should go to the bathroom like decent folks would." The asshole wasn't backing down.

"Yes, because they would be so comfortable feeding babies while sitting on toilet seats. It's a freaking hospital." Ally was so sick of hypocrisy. "They tell you to breastfeed and then make it hard on the mom."

She realized everyone was looking at her. Eric and the guys from Top were in with Macon, but Macon's family was all sitting in those chairs and every eye was glued to her. Except the babies. They were occupied.

"You stay out of this, missy," the man said. "I have rights and I shouldn't have to see women running around showing off their titties like it's a *Girls Gone Wild* film."

"Seriously? This is *Girls Gone Wild*, asshole." She flashed him. She'd taken off her bra the night before. She hadn't exactly been able to slip it on in front of Macon and his brother.

The man gasped and then practically ran out of the room.

The volunteer breathed a sigh of relief. "Oh, thank god. That big guy over there scares the hell out of me. I think he was about to come over here. I was actually going to run and hide in the bathroom. I don't get paid to handle this."

Ally smoothed down her shirt. Yep, she'd flashed her boobs in front of Macon's friends and family. She was all kinds of classy.

She glanced over and instead of looks of horror, she got thumbs-ups and wide grins.

"Oh, my god. I can't believe you did that." Deena was laughing her ass off.

"You've got very nice breasts, young lady," the woman with the cane said primly. "If you want to keep them that way, you should wear a bra. My poor sister's drag the floor and she never wore a bra."

Ally felt a hand on her shoulder and turned, praying security wasn't about to escort her out. Instead, she got Macon's smiling brother.

"Oh, you're going to be trouble. I think you'll fit right in." He drew her into a hug. "Did I thank you for saving my brother?"

It took her a second, but she hugged him back. She missed this, missed having anyone who was happy to see her, who liked her. Even the last few months with her mother she'd felt more like a caregiver than a beloved daughter. "No problem."

He drew her into the waiting room and began to introduce her.

She'd never imagined flashing could be such a great icebreaker.

CHAPTER FOUR

Macon finished the cake with a final swipe of his hand. Dark chocolate with a ganache icing. It would be served with a homemade vanilla bean ice cream that hopefully he still had enough of. Ally proved fond of his ice cream. She'd watched him make it with liquid nitrogen, her eyes widening when the smoke had gone everywhere.

The door to the kitchen came open and Ally walked through wearing faded jeans and one of those soft T-shirts she always seemed to wear that hugged her breasts in all the right places. Her eyes were wide as she strode in. Ally, he'd learned, did everything with a sort of anxious energy. It was hard for her to stay still. "That is a roomful of babies. They're everywhere. I want to roll around in them."

"It's going to be a roomful of poop in about twenty minutes." His living room was being used as a nursery. It was the reason the "gang" was using Adam's place. He had a large playroom and he was the only one with a guesthouse to stash the babies in.

"They're not free-range babies, so it should be all right." Ally stopped to admire the cake. "This is beautiful. You have to teach me how to do the roses."

"I will. I'm doing a cake for an anniversary party next week. You can help me." He'd started to teach her some of the finer points of his job. She seemed fascinated with cake decorating. He'd taught her the art of writing with a pastry bag. He'd also started thinking longer term. He no longer questioned whether she would be here next week. "And thank god they're not free range."

She grinned. "Don't want to clean up that mess, huh? So who are the two women they have watching the kiddos?"

"They're actually Dr. Daley's sisters. Nice ladies. Laurel and Lisa."

"And they babysit?"

"They're sub…substitutes. Substitute teachers. They make money on the side this way." He'd almost explained that the young women were training as submissives at Sanctum, Big Tag's club. Well, it had been his club before it was blown up by an asswipe traitor who should have his entrails ground into dust and shoved up his anal cavity without lube. Tag's words, not his. Apparently the dude was dead, but Macon wasn't so sure that would stop Big Tag. If he thought he could properly punish a corpse, he might do it. The new Sanctum was under construction.

"They're substitutes? Seriously? One of them was talking about working for a law firm. She said babysitting wasn't a big thing because she had to deal with shit all day long and at least babies are cute. When do we need to get the cake over? And what about the appetizers? Should I be at the big house heating them up?"

She would have to go to the big house since there was absolutely no heat in this house. None. No making out. No cuddling. For five days she'd babied him, making sure he ate healthy and got enough water. She'd made him stay in bed the whole first day and kept him from working out. She'd driven him to physical therapy and then nagged the therapist about making him do too much.

Not once had she kissed him or even said a thing that would make him think she wanted him to kiss her. They ate together, watched TV together, cooked together.

They were roommates.

"Don't worry about it. Adam's going to finish the apps and Serena has all the salads. It's only a little buffet."

"A little? It's magnificent. I can't wait to see it. Do you think they'll mind if I sneak a plate? I promise to hide in the kitchen. We should get catering uniforms. You know, black pants, white shirt. They could come in handy."

"You're not going." He'd thought about it that first day. He'd thought about the fact that he could take her over to the mini club the McKay-Taggart group had set up and he could watch her. He could see if she had any interest at all. Of course, that was when he'd thought they would at least have had a heavy make-out session by this point. Now that he realized she was simply looking for a place to stay and a bit of friendship, he thought taking her to watch his friends have sex in kinky ways was probably a mistake.

God, he wanted to have sex with her in kinky ways. Hell, he'd take straight up vanilla. Being close to her for days was killing him. She wore boxer shorts and a tank top to bed and she would walk out of her room in the morning with her hair all mussed and her sleepy eyes and he would put a cup of coffee in her hand, and all he could think about were her nipples. Until she turned around and then he thought about her ass.

She required two cups of strong coffee to get her going in the mornings. She particularly liked the Sumatra blend. He hadn't told her he was experimenting, but he changed the blend until he found the one that made her sigh and lick her lips. By the time she was awake, he was putting an egg white omelet with whatever veg they had on hand and a bowl of fresh fruit in front of her. She'd been surprised at how healthy he ate. He'd explained that he was a pastry chef. Everything else had to be healthy or he'd weigh a ton.

"You don't need any help tonight?"

He shook his head. "I'm going to drop off the cake and then I'll come back over and we can play with the babies."

A frown creased her forehead. "But I heard you talking to Adam about how you were looking forward to this."

That had been when he'd still had hope that he might participate. Even if it was only in a voyeuristic fashion. "I'm taking the night off."

Her eyes narrowed and he was really worried she could see past his layers of skin right down to his soul. She turned without another word and walked back out of the kitchen. He should have let it go, pleased that she wasn't questioning him any more.

But he'd started to know that look. That look in Ally's eyes meant trouble. He followed.

"How's the substitute teaching business these days, ladies?"

Shit. And shit. And more shit. "Ally…"

Laurel was holding one of the babies. One of the ones who wasn't Tristan. He knew his nephew but the other babies all kind of looked alike. Tristan was currently pulling his baby body up on the sofa. He grinned, showing one tiny tooth.

"Uhm, I've never done that. That sounds perfectly horrible," Laurel said with a shudder. "I'm a paralegal."

She pointed back to him. "That one said you were watching the babies because you're subs who need extra money."

Lisa shook her head as she laid one of the twins down in the traveling bassinet the Taggarts had set up twenty minutes ago. "Oh, no, he meant we're in submissive training."

And that was the way his night went to shit. "I wasn't going to tell her that. You two need to learn what 'private club' means."

Lisa winced. "I'm sorry, Sir."

Laurel looked between the two of them. "I apologize. I assumed she would know what a sub is given the fact that she lives with you, Sir."

"Submissive?" Ally said the word in that way that let him know she kind of knew what it meant but wasn't exactly rah-rah about it.

Macon looked at Lisa and Laurel. He wasn't really mad at them. They should be safe to talk here. He was the one who had screwed up. "I'm sorry, ladies. You're right. I should have told her. Can you explain why you're here?"

Laurel patted the baby's back. "Sanctum has a training program for Doms and subs. The actual club costs are way too expensive for either of us, but Big Tag has a program where he lets us in if we help out where we can. Subs end up watching kiddos a lot. Well, the ones who like kids. Normally Vince would be with us, but he's doing a play in Austin this week. He's an actor and a total bottom. He's got a great touch with Carys. She gets crabby. All the Doms in training are helping with the Sanctum rebuild."

"After what I did with a jigsaw, they won't let me near the construction," Lisa explained.

Ally turned on him, pointing back to the kitchen. "Talk. Now."

He stopped and crossed his arms over his chest because that tone did not sit right with him. He was always polite with her. He'd spent a week taking care of her, too. He'd done the marriage where his wife pushed him around. He wasn't about to start that again.

She'd been walking toward the kitchen but stopped in her tracks when she realized he hadn't moved. "What?"

"You should be more polite," Laurel said in a singsong voice. She was bouncing a baby. "Shouldn't she, Aidan? Yes, she should show some respect."

She stopped for a minute and then turned back to him. "Could I talk to you in the kitchen, please?"

He nodded and followed her back, not looking forward to the next couple of minutes. Maybe she wouldn't be here next week.

When he pushed through the kitchen door, she was leaning against the island. "Submissives? Doms?"

"My brother is into alternative lifestyles and as he is your host, I expect you to treat him with a modicum of respect." He owed his brother. His brother had spent a lifetime with people judging him. He wasn't going to bring another person into Adam's life who might misunderstand him.

She frowned his way. "I haven't been disrespectful to Adam."

"And to me?" He'd done nothing to earn that glare from earlier or the way she'd hauled him in front of the Daley girls.

"Oh, god, you're one of them."

He was done. He had a job to do. He crossed to the island and started gathering the things he would need. "I'll be back after the party. I'm sorry about the disturbance, but the babies should be gone sometime after midnight."

The kitchen got quiet as he started organizing his things.

He felt a hand on his back and then Ally spoke quietly. "I'm sorry. I didn't mean to offend you."

"It's not a problem." Maybe he was more invested than he thought. He really didn't like the way she'd reacted. It bugged him. He could handle her ordering him around when it came to healthcare. That felt like caring. This felt too much like judgment, and he wasn't going to take that again.

"I'm sorry."

He took a deep breath and really meant it when he said it this time. "It's all right."

It wasn't her fault she couldn't deal with his lifestyle choices. He hadn't exactly talked to her about it. They'd spent the week chatting about inconsequential things. He knew she liked to watch mystery movies and read romances, and he'd talked about the fact that he loved reading thrillers. They'd spent an enormous amount of time in the kitchen where he felt the most comfortable. He'd avoided talking about his past. She was glib when she talked about hers. Now that he looked at it, they hadn't been serious at all.

Roommates. They hadn't tried to be anything more and maybe that was all right. He didn't want to get involved with a woman who didn't want to know him. He'd already been married to one.

"It doesn't feel all right," she said in a quiet voice.

"It's not a big deal. I'm sorry I didn't explain it to you before. The party earlier was for Grace's family. This one is for Grace's friends. Her kink family, if you will. I'll handle everything. I have to make sure Serena and Adam know how to reheat if they need to. My brother is actually quite good in the kitchen, too." He politely broke her hold and stepped away. If they weren't going to be more than friends, he didn't think it was appropriate to get intimate. He also didn't want a quick hookup or a "friends with benefits" type thing with her.

"Sean is involved, too," she said quietly. "That's why he called the restaurant Top. I thought it was because he wanted to be the top restaurant, but that wasn't what he meant."

He looked back at her. She was leaning against the fridge, her arms crossed over her chest. He kept the island between them, giving her space since it looked like she'd gone back into protective mode. "It's not something you have to worry about. Sean's a good guy."

"He hits his wife."

That felt like a kick in the gut. Well, it was better to know sooner than later. "They play together. Everything they do is mutually agreed on and for her pleasure. Does Grace look like an abused woman?"

She shook her head as though trying to clear it. "Could you give me a minute? I'm trying to wrap my brain around it."

This was what his brother had to deal with all these years. "You don't have to. It has nothing to do with you. It doesn't hurt you or anyone. It's people choosing to live and play together. If you can't handle that, the door is that way, but if you think I'm going to stand here and debate with you whether Sean and my brother are abusive husbands because they and their wives indulge in spanking and bondage, you're wrong. I won't justify myself or my family to you."

Tears had formed in her eyes and it took everything he had to stand his ground and not reverse everything he'd said. She stood there as the tears fell on her cheek, but she wasn't looking at him. She was staring at a place on the floor as though she couldn't stand to look at him. As if he was going to turn into some kind of monster.

He forced himself to move. He grabbed the cake plate and started readying Grace's birthday cake for transfer.

"He went to a lot of trouble for her. Two parties for her birthday," she mentioned quietly.

"He loves her. You should see what Big Tag does for his wife. Who is also his sub."

"And you want to have that kind of relationship?"

He sealed the cake in and prayed he made it across the yard without tripping. He'd almost lost a plate of petit fours for the family party when he'd tried to take a shortcut to Bessie. God, he was calling her car by that name now, too. Ally had saved the little cakes. She'd been walking right next to him, chatting away. He hadn't realized how closely she'd been watching him.

He was going to miss their easy friendship. He'd been thinking bitterly about it before, but now he realized how lonely he was going to be without her. He would have taken her friendship without the sex if that was all he could have. A heaviness set over him.

"I've never had that kind of relationship. I've been training and I like it. I enjoy feeling like I have control somewhere. I like feeling like someone needs me even if it's only for a while. But that doesn't matter. I won't hit you, Ally, if that's what you're really asking. I won't hurt you or try to force you to do anything you don't want to do. Look, if knowing this about me makes you uncomfortable staying here, then let me loan you some money to get your own place. I don't have much but I can float you a down payment and first month's rent. You can pay me back in installments."

"You want me to leave?"

"No, but I don't want you to be afraid of me and I think you are right now. You don't have to decide tonight. I'll stay over at the big house and we can talk about it in the morning." He picked up the cake. "Don't forget to lock the deadbolt." He turned to go and thought about having a beer. His brother would have a fridge full of it, but he would only have one. He was going to do his job and ensure everything was all right with the play party and then he'd hit the guest room and sit up all night wondering how he was going to miss a person he'd only known for a few weeks.

Her arms went around his waist and she plastered her front to his back. "Please don't go. Not like this."

"Ally, it's all right. I'm not going to kick you out. It's okay."

She didn't let go. If anything, her hold tightened. "I'm not afraid of you. I know you wouldn't hurt me. And I know Sean and Adam are good men. Please don't be mad at me. I didn't expect it and I had a bad reaction and I'm sorry. I get stuck in a corner sometimes and I'm too stubborn to come out. I don't want to leave here. I don't want to leave you."

"What is this really about?" It felt bigger than a misunderstanding. He set the cake down because it looked like this conversation was going to take a while.

She was quiet for a moment, her head resting against his back. "My dad hit my mom. He was a mean drunk. She left when I was eight. I wished she'd taken me with her. He didn't smack me around, but he would scare the crap out of me. That's when I started running away."

He'd wondered. She was so glib that she had to be glossing over something bad. He let his hand drift to where she was holding on to him like a lifeline. "No one's going to hurt you here, baby."

He probably shouldn't have used the endearment. She wasn't his baby, but he wanted to give her some affection and words were likely the only way she would take it from him.

She slowly let go and he turned around. Her face was red, and he knew telling him that truth about herself had cost her. He didn't want to hurt her. Not physically. Not emotionally. She was so strong and he hated to see her looking vulnerable. The last time he'd seen her like this was when Timothy had assaulted her. He kept his hands to his sides despite the fact that he wanted to hold her. "It's all right. You don't have to talk anymore. It's okay."

She walked right into his arms like she belonged there. She put her head against his chest, her body flush to his. She wasn't trying to put distance between them or show him that they could still be friendly. This was an all-out plea for comfort, and he couldn't deny her. He sighed as his arms wrapped around her and their bodies fit together for the first time in days.

This was where he'd needed to be. This was what he'd wanted. He'd wanted to be able to smell her shampoo and feel her body nestled to his, but it was confusing.

"Ally, I don't understand. Baby, you're going to have to tell me what you want from me because I can't read your mind. I've kept my hands to myself all week because it seems like you only want to be friends, but I have to say, it feels like more right now. If I'm reading you wrong, I would like for you to tell me. I care about you. A lot. If you don't feel the same way, please tell me. It doesn't mean we can't be friends. It doesn't mean you can't stay here. I simply need to adjust my expectations."

Her head moved against his chest like she was trying to find the right spot. She settled her ear right over his heart. "Have you ever wanted something, but you know you probably can't have it?"

"Baby, I haven't been playing coy. If you want me all you have to do is ask." He smoothed a hand down her hair, enjoying the rich feel of it. Like spun silk. "But you should know that while I don't have to top you to have a relationship with you, all my friends are into the lifestyle. If that's going to bother you, maybe we should talk about it."

"Or maybe you should show me and I'll promise to try not to let the fact that my dad was an atrocious human being ruin this, too." Her face turned up, her eyes still shining with tears. "I'm not usually like this, Macon. I promise. I'm not so damaged that I can't have a relationship. And I know I pulled back this week, but I wanted you to know me. I thought it was a bad idea to jump into bed with you. I didn't want to be just another woman you went to bed with."

"Uhm, baby, you seem to have gotten the wrong impression of me. I haven't been to bed with anyone but my right hand in well over a year and honestly, there hasn't even been much of that. I was stationed in Afghanistan and then I came home to divorce papers. So you wouldn't be another woman. You would be one of two."

Her eyes widened. "Two?"

He nodded and kind of wished he was the stud she thought he was. He was about to ruin that impression. "I married Elise when I was eighteen. I've never slept with anyone else. So if you're looking for an incredible amount of experience, you won't find it with me. You should know that. After the accident, well, there aren't a lot of women out there looking for a broke, divorced, one-legged veteran."

"One and a quarter legs. We have to use all our assets, Miles." She went up on her toes. "I want you so badly. I don't think I've ever wanted a man the way I want you. I want to be enough for you."

It was all he could possibly have asked for. He leaned over and brushed their lips together. "You are. And you don't need to come with me. Like I said, I don't need to top you to be with you. I'll drop the cake off and come back here. We'll play with the kids and maybe later tonight we'll make out and see where things go. I don't want to push you. This relationship is important to me."

She hugged him again. "It's important to me, too. And that's why I want to go. I want to see. Will they let me watch? Or will they think I'm a total perv for wanting to watch?"

"Oh, that house is full of happy perverts right now." He sighed, hoping he wasn't making a mistake. "I'd already asked if I could bring you. Big Tag agreed. You're welcome, but you're coming in with me and that means there are some rules."

"Do I call you Sir? I caught that, you know." At least she sounded happy again.

"No. You call me Macon and you stay close to me. If I give you an order, it's for your safety and the safety of the others. This is a private play party. There are going to be different scenes going on in various rooms of the house, though most people will be in the dungeon. And there will be naked people. If this was Sanctum, you wouldn't be allowed to come in street clothes."

"I don't have anything sexy."

"You're sexy exactly the way you are." He loved her in jeans and a T-shirt or her Top uniform or her PJs.

"You say the sweetest things, Miles." She glanced back up at him and gave him a tremulous smile. "I'm crazy about you. I want this to work."

He cupped her cheeks and held her still for a long kiss. He molded his lips to hers, going slow and savoring every moment. He couldn't ask for more than an honest chance with her. "I'm crazy about you, too."

He dipped his head down again. The cake could wait a few minutes more.

* * * *

She clung to Macon's hand and it wasn't really about being afraid. She could finally hold it. She could finally feel their fingers threading together. She moved closer to him as they ventured out of the dining room after putting the finishing touches on the buffet. It was gorgeous. Macon hadn't made everything, but in her mind his were the tastiest. In addition to the cake and a plate of tiny lemon angel food cakes with a dash of lemon confit, he'd made three types of hummus, put together a charcuterie board and a cheese plate, and a lovely selection of crudités. She'd helped him with the variety of vegetables, cutting them the way he taught her to.

She loved living with Macon. She was fairly certain she was falling in love with Macon. Maybe it was a mistake, maybe she was being naïve, but he couldn't have hurt her brother. She wanted the truth, but she was no longer sure she wanted it at the price of her relationship with him.

"Are you ready? There's a bar set up in the living room, but no one will be drunk here. Big Tag would never allow that. There's a two drink max."

"Really?"

"Discipline is the name of the game with this crowd," Macon explained. "They can't take care of their subs if they drink too much and they always take care of their subs. And here are our first naked people. Naturally it's my sister-in-law. Yeah, I had to get used to that."

Ally felt her jaw drop. Serena Dean-Miles, the mild-mannered writer she'd gotten to know over the last week, was trussed up like a turkey and all she was wearing was some rope. It looked like quite a bit of rope, but it didn't cover anything important. Her arms were bound behind her back, her breasts proudly displayed in what looked like the reverse version of a bra since her torso was covered but her breasts were left bare.

"Who didn't get her word count in, today?" Adam asked, his voice a low growl. She had to admit that Macon's big brother looked fine wearing nothing but what appeared to be a pair of leather pants. His chest was perfectly sculpted, every inch of him lean muscle.

"It was me, Master," Serena said. Gone were her glasses and her typical bun. Her brown and blonde hair flowed around, making her look feminine and sexy. She bit her bottom lip and looked up at Adam with big eyes. "I'm so sorry. I didn't have enough time today."

"She's not really sorry," Ally whispered to Macon.

Macon grinned at her. "She might be in a minute, but it's all play. They set up this scene weeks ago. They like to call it the 'naughty author gives in to her muses.'"

She couldn't help but giggle at that. Did they really sit around and plan a thing like this? She tried to picture the three of them sitting around the dinner table talking about what kind of things they would use. Toys, she corrected. They would talk about what toys they would use when they played. Or maybe they would talk about it in bed. Maybe they would hold each other and talk about their fantasies.

Did she have any sexual fantasies? All of her dreams revolved around Macon, but it was more about him holding her and kissing her. She'd kind of thought she would get through the sex in order to enjoy the cuddling.

What if she could have more?

Jacob Dean stepped up. Like his partner, he wore nothing but a pair of leather pants and boots. He carried a crop in his hands. He stepped in front of Serena and lightly tapped her breasts. "And what was our favorite author doing when she should have been writing?"

"Thinking about my plot," Serena replied.

That earned her a hard smack on her backside from Adam. The sound cracked through the air. It made Ally jump, but Macon's arms came around her, pulling her into the warmth and safety of his body. "It's all right. She's okay."

"I know," she forced herself to say.

Macon's deep voice rumbled in her ear. "Watch her. She winces, but she doesn't try to wriggle away. The sound is worse than the sensation. I've heard Serena quite likes the sensation."

Jake brought the crop down on her backside again. Serena did wiggle a little, but toward her husband. She definitely wasn't trying to get away.

"Do you want to try that again, love?" Jacob asked. "I could always get out the ginger lube."

Apparently Serena didn't like flavored lube because she couldn't get the words out fast enough. "I was on Facebook and then I played way too much Candy Crush. I'm so sorry, Master. Please don't spank me again. I'll be good. You really shouldn't spank me with that crop."

It sounded believable and for a moment Ally stiffened, hearing some of the words that had come from her mother's mouth, but then Serena looked up and the brightest smile hit her face.

"Hey, Allyson. I'm so glad you could make it," she said, sounding completely like Serena again.

Adam squinted out and then smiled, too. He gave her a wave. "Hey, nice to see you."

Jake frowned at his partner and their wife. He put one hand on his hip as the crop tapped against his outer thigh. "Do you two remember anything about sceneing? Anything at all? Has the whole parenting thing turned us into that threesome? You know, the one that can't concentrate on their scene and makes everyone crazy?"

Adam seemed utterly unfazed by the Dom's stare. "I was surprised to see her here. I thought she was going to go all Anastasia Steele on us."

"Good one, babe. I'd high-five you if Jake wasn't so good with the knots," Serena replied.

"I'm about to remind you how good I am with a crop." Jake's arm went up and came back down, the crop hitting Serena's backside.

Serena gasped but Ally couldn't miss the way she winked her way right before going back into her naughty author mode. Jake and Adam took turns "torturing" her.

Macon kept her close, an arm around her at all times. She leaned against him, reveling in his warmth and strength. She'd started watching the scene with a deep anxiety, but each moment that went by she relaxed a bit more. Serena would look over every now and then and give her a smile or a wink, as though she knew it was hard for her.

How much had they figured out about her background? Was she that transparent? She prided herself on never showing her pain. Only the thought of losing Macon had forced her to talk today. For a moment, when she'd been in his arms, it had been okay to talk about it, to let herself feel it one more time and let a tiny piece of the pain go.

Macon leaned over. "They are about to get to the sexual part where my brother shows off his junk. This is where I take my leave."

Naturally he wanted to leave before the good part, but she let him lead her away. She didn't even try to take a peek.

He led her down the hallway. It looked like the whole house had been turned into a decadent palace complete with low lighting and thudding music that fed through the home's speaker system. It was transformed from the airy, filled-with-light home she knew from eating lunches or dinners with the family. Everywhere she looked there were men and women in various states of undress. The women wore corsets and tiny thongs or skirts that really didn't cover much. There were lots of stilettos and plenty of bare feet. She stopped as she watched a woman on a leash. She stared, looking for signs that she didn't like the leash.

"If that woman didn't like her leash, she would break it and put her husband on his ass," Macon whispered in her ear.

Once more, she had the feeling of being completely transparent to these people. Maybe she'd been rude. "Sorry."

"No, they don't mind you watching. If they weren't comfortable with others watching they wouldn't be here, but you have to get it through your head that these aren't women who are being abused. They're women who made a choice a long time ago about who they want to be. The woman on the leash is Karina Brighton. Her husband is a Dallas police lieutenant and former Green Beret, and he wouldn't try to take her in a fight. She submits to him because she finds it relaxing and pleasurable for both of them. That leash and collar are there for play. The way I heard, Karina lost a bet and Derek forced her to try puppy play and surprise, she kind of liked it."

Even as he spoke, the big Dom sat down on one of the couches in the designated lounge area of the house.

"So she pretends to be a puppy? Does she sit at his feet?"

"I'm sure she does from time to time, but I think he wants this particular puppy on his lap." He chuckled as the Dom lightly tugged on his sub's leash and pulled her into his lap. His hands went over her hair and he stroked her. She cuddled up in his arms as he started speaking softly to another Dom and sub who seemed very cozy.

What would it feel like to be able to cuddle up to Macon and feel completely and utterly like she belonged in his arms? What would it feel like to do it without any secrets between them?

She'd left it too late. She couldn't tell him the truth now. She would lose him.

"Hey, are you all right?"

She'd gone stiff again, her shoulders up around her ears. He thought she was scared. She forced herself to relax and gave him a smile. "I'm good."

His hand found hers. "Are you ready for more?"

She was ready to spend as much time with him as she possibly could. She nodded and he led her down the hall.

Three hours later, she helped Serena pack up the last of the food. Big Tag had casually snatched up the lemon cakes before heading across the property with his wife to pick up their babies. He'd also gifted Grace with a gorgeous Tiffany bracelet for her birthday, so Ally didn't think anyone minded. Grace and Sean had looked completely satisfied with their evening and had even come over to tell Ally how happy they'd been to see her there.

She'd watched all manner of loving perversion and it was making her think.

"Did we freak you out?" Serena asked as she closed the lid on a container of hummus.

"Only the guy with the whip," Ally replied honestly.

Serena nodded. "Yeah, when Kai gets the right sub, he can really go at it. Maia is a pain slut. She's also a truly horrible human being, so she's the perfect person to set off Kai's inner sadist."

"They're a couple?" They'd been the only thing she hadn't eventually warmed to. There was something cold about the way they'd been, as though there hadn't been love between them.

"Oh, no. Kai can't stand Maia and she sees him as a means to an end. It's not all hearts and flowers and perfectly placed butt plugs. Sometimes it's simply about getting something you need. It's like that for a lot of single people who play. They come to Sanctum to let off steam in a controlled way that brings someone else what they need. Kai has a strong sadist streak. He controls it by finding partners who enjoy the pain he gives them."

He'd been gorgeous, a blond god of a man in leather, but he made her shiver a bit. "Holy shit, he's like the Dom version of Dexter."

Serena nodded. "I'm so using that in a book. I'm sure Kai would describe it in more technical, psychological terms. He's the resident shrink. If you had been coming into Sanctum and not a private party, you would have to be cleared by Kai first. Everyone in the club gets to meet with Kai to make sure they're here for the right reasons."

Ally felt her jaw drop. "He's a shrink? The dude with the whip?"

"Yep. His specialty is PTSD in war vets."

Macon had mentioned a Kai. He'd talked about seeing him. It was a freaky world where the guy with the whip was helping everyone else with their sanity situations.

But then again, maybe it was a freaky world period.

"Hey, Serena, where's the vacuum? I've got the living room back to normal. It just needs a sweep." Speak of the devil. Kai Ferguson was standing in the kitchen wearing a perfectly normal pair of jeans and a T-shirt that hugged his lean frame. His sandy blond hair was pulled back in a queue and he had a pair of glasses on that did nothing to hide his hotness factor. He smiled her way and it was an open, honest smile that looked nothing like the gleam of sadistic glee in his eyes from earlier in the evening. "Hi. You're Macon's girl, Ally, right?"

Being called Macon's girl kind of made her beam inside. She held a hand out. "Allyson Jones."

"Kai Ferguson. I've been hoping to meet you." He took her hand and shook it before stepping back. "I'll talk to Macon about setting up an appointment."

"What? Why?" She had to admit that he still scared her a bit.

"This was a private party. Didn't Macon explain?"

"Macon is going slow with the new girl," Macon said as he walked in. He looked at Kai. "Macon is trying not to scare the new girl off."

Kai put a hand up. "Hey, I'm only doing my job. You know she can't come to Sanctum without my clearance. Oh, Sanctum might move around from house to house right now, but the rules are the same. I know Big Tag will probably tell me to clear her because you're the almighty pie maker, but it's best if we all follow the rules."

"She doesn't even know if any of this stuff is for her yet," Macon argued.

Kai turned his gaze her way. "Did any of the scenes sexually arouse you?"

She felt her whole face go hot.

"Dude," Macon protested.

Kai shook his head, obviously unwilling to concede his point. "Well, if she can't even talk about sex then she probably has no place in a sex club. I'm not trying to be a dick, but I do have to decide if she belongs here. People come to Sanctum for a judgment-free place to indulge their personalities and their kinks. I watched her tonight. She seemed a bit on edge, like she was disturbed. I wasn't the only one who noticed."

Humiliation swept through her. "I'm sorry. I didn't mean to make anyone uncomfortable."

Serena moved to her side. "You didn't, sweetie."

"She did," Kai said matter of factly. "I was actually surprised that this was the girl who flashed an entire waiting room. When they described you to me, I kind of thought you'd be a free spirit."

"Kai, don't," Macon warned. "I know what you're doing."

"Then you should know I'm helping."

It didn't feel like he was helping. "That was impulsive." And it had felt good. Why couldn't she talk about it? Why was her sexuality less important than everyone else's? Kai "Dexter" Ferguson was kind of making her mad, and that made her want to answer his question. "And yes, I did get sexually aroused and yes, some of it was disturbing and it still aroused me."

Kai's smile was so wide, it lit up his whole face. "See, there you go. Now you know you've got some kink in you. Everyone does. Most people simply don't acknowledge it. What disturbed you? I know I did."

Damn him. He'd known what he was doing, but it seemed stubborn not to talk now. "The violence bothered me because of some things that happened when I was a kid."

"All right. That's a trigger for you. You can either avoid even watching scenes like that or we can work on it. The good news is Macon's not that kind of a top. He's a very indulgent top. I doubt he even truly enjoys spanking a woman."

"I totally like spanking a woman and when the hell did this turn into a therapy session?" Macon shook his head and leaned against the counter.

"There's never a bad time for a therapy session, my friend. I'm hopeful for you. You've smiled more since this woman came into your life. I want to help you make it work. Relationships, like anything in life, require more than luck, more than simply love. They require two people who honestly want to be together, who are willing to work through the issues that will inevitably try to keep them apart. It's not easy to take two independent beings and form a really workable couple."

Serena cleared her throat.

"Or three," Kai allowed before turning back to Ally. "I saw you two watching the scene but there wasn't a lot of talk between you. You held hands, but I don't feel the real intimacy. You're not sleeping together."

"Has anyone ever told you you're a busybody, Kai?" Macon asked, obviously irritated.

"It's a hobby. This is about being your friend and not your therapist. You're sad you're not sleeping with her. I would be sad, too. She's a gorgeous woman." Kai gave her a polite nod.

She'd landed in some weird place. At home, no one ever talked about sex. That might be why she'd never had any really good sex.

Whatever her new friends were, she could tell one thing. They were happy.

"I'm afraid to sleep with him," she admitted. "Not because he would hurt me. I know he never would. I'm afraid I would be disappointing. I would rather have him in my life without sex than out of it because I wasn't enough."

Macon turned to her. "Babe, that's not how it works."

Kai was grinning from ear to ear, like a little boy who'd been given a present. "Why would you think you aren't enough?"

"Is it because you're not a screaming orgasmer?" Serena asked. "That's the guy's fault, you know. Maybe you haven't had a decent lover yet."

"It's not always the guy's fault," Kai disagreed. "What do you think about during sex, Ally?"

Macon sighed as though he knew where the shrink was going.

She didn't know where any of this was going. "Uhm, I don't know. It depends on what's going on in my life. Sometimes I think about what he's doing and that it's not working, and sometimes I think about what I need to do the next day. I worry a lot."

"If her brain works like her body, then she never stops thinking," Macon explained. "She's always moving. Even when we sit and watch TV, she's doing something else. She'll knit or make lists of things to do. She's never still."

"I've always been that way." She'd never seen that there was anything wrong with it.

"She's anxious. You need to get her out of her head. Why don't you come by my place and we can have a session?" Kai offered. "I can fit you in on Tuesday. We'll probably need an hour or two."

"I think I can handle this, buddy." Macon patted his friend on the shoulder and then looked to Serena. "Do you mind if we head out?"

Serena shook her head. "Of course not." She enveloped Ally in a hug. "It was so good to have you here. Jake went over and got Tristan. I think you two are now baby free."

"Call me if you need anything," Kai offered.

Macon chuckled at that and took her hand. "Come on, babe. We need to talk."

She let him lead her out, scared to death of what they were about to do.

CHAPTER FIVE

Macon locked the door behind him and the house was beautifully still. After all the excitement of the night, it was good to come home to quiet and peace. The Daley girls had eradicated any sign that their home had been used as a nursery and everything was back to its neat, peaceful state.

So why was his body humming with energy?

He was only going to talk to her. Kai was right about that. They needed to talk. Sure it would be so much easier to fall into bed and enjoy whatever they could find, but he'd done that before. He wanted more with Ally. So only talk. And maybe some kissing. Hey, if she wanted more, he would give it to her. But if she only needed to talk, he would do that instead. Why was he so damn nervous?

"Do you want some coffee?"

She looked up at him, a pink flush to her cheeks. "You know most guys would offer a girl wine or a drink at this point."

He shook his head. Did she really think he hadn't noticed her habits? "You don't drink."

"But you do. I've seen you drink with Eric and the guys."

"I don't if it makes you uncomfortable." There was a six-pack of beer sitting in the fridge. It had been there since the day before the tornado.

She bit her bottom lip and crossed her arms over her chest.

"Sometimes I think you're too good to be true."

"You're the only person in the world who thinks that. Are we ready? I'd like to talk about something important. We've spent a week talking about movies and books and not a thing about our real selves, and that's what got us in trouble earlier today."

She turned and walked to the couch and sat down. "Okay."

She said it like talking would be an unpleasant experience. He was starting to understand that talking wasn't easy for Ally. It was easier for him since he'd spent months in therapy with Kai. He'd figured out a couple of weeks into his Dallas residence that talking about things didn't make him less of a man. He'd reevaluated everything about what it meant to be a man since he'd come to Dallas. He sat down on the sofa beside her.

"Do you want to go to bed with me?"

"Yes." At least she didn't hesitate answering that question.

"Good. I want to take the next step with you, too. You're scared that you won't be enough for me. Well, I'm scared I'm not very good in bed. I know I'm supposed to be some kind of alpha male who never questions that he's sex on two legs, but I'm damaged here and I'm really tired of pretending I'm not human. I would very much like to be able to be human with you."

Her whole body seemed to soften and she reached for his hand. "Why would you think that?"

He let her take it, enjoying the warmth. "Because my wife told me I was useless with two legs so I would be completely pathetic with one. She was having an affair with my brother. Not Adam, obviously. Alan. He's my brother, the firstborn and our father's favorite. Dad disowned Adam because of the kink. I wasn't exactly disowned. I walked away. I could go back if I accepted my brother's new girlfriend. Who happens to be my old wife. Yeah, we're fucked up."

Her hand slid over his and then back again as though she was trying to soothe him. "Everyone is, I think. Some people are simply better at hiding it. What if we tried? I mean, we're never going to know if we have chemistry if we don't try."

"Oh, we have chemistry, baby. At least on my side we do. I get hard when you walk in a room."

"Really?"

At least here honesty worked for her. "Oh yeah. Do you remember that first day you showed up at Top and you were all stuttery and out of sorts? I let you inside and you waited with me until Sean could see you."

"I remember you were making a chocolate glaze for poached pears and you let me try it."

"Yep, I had a hard-on." He shifted back, getting comfortable, though it meant letting go of her hand. "I kind of have one now."

Kind of was understating it. His cock was rock hard and desperate, but he was determined to give her the time she needed.

Her gaze went down to his crotch and her eyes went wide. "You're serious."

"Yes, but I'm not going to do anything about it until you're ready."

She groaned. "You're killing me, Miles. Why can't you be like every other guy in the freaking world and jump on me? Why do you have to make it hard?"

He put a bit of bite in his tone. Her brat wasn't needed here tonight. "Because I take this seriously. If you want a quick fuck, you should probably find someone else."

She flushed. "I'm sorry, Macon. I am ready. And I've thought about it and I want to put this in your hands. I want you to be in control of this because I don't know what I'm doing and honestly, I don't even know what I really want except to feel close to you."

"I know what I want." It felt good to be honest with someone for a change.

"What's that?"

"I want to make you scream. I want to be the man who shows you how hot you can get because I think you could burn, baby. You simply have to trust me. You have to let go and stop thinking about anything but what you're feeling." Kai might be a busybody, but he had gotten to the heart of the matter. She thought too much. She was in constant protection mode and he needed her to let those walls down. "I want to do some sensation play with you. It doesn't have to end in sex."

It would likely end in a massive masturbation session if she said no. His right hand was going to get some tonight.

"All right. What do you want me to do?"

He stood up and held out a hand. "Let's go to your bedroom." It would be easier to walk away from her than it would be to watch her walk away. Besides, she might feel more comfortable around her own things. "Do you have a scarf?"

"Sure. It's in my room." Her hand was trembling when she placed it in his.

He helped her up and held her hand to his chest. "Baby, I know you gave me control, but you understand how this works, right? You're giving me control to bring you pleasure but the minute you feel unsafe, tell me and I stop."

She went up on her toes and brushed her mouth against his. "Like I said. Too good to be true."

"You wouldn't say that if you'd seen me a few months ago." He started to lead her back to the bedroom. He sure as hell didn't want her to think he was some kind of saint. "I was drunk all the time and I was bitter and angry."

"After you lost your leg? And your wife left you? I can understand that. I might have been homicidal, Macon."

She would have gone after Elise with her hammer very likely. He enjoyed her crazy streak. He'd grown up around women like his stepmother. Pretty, perfect, cold. It wasn't until he'd actually gone into the Army that he met some real women. He'd thought he needed a female like Elise who wanted to be an officer's wife. Her father had connections through his law firm. Her mother had been a model socialite. Macon's stepmother had handpicked Elise.

If Ally had been his wife, he wouldn't have woken up alone in a hospital room in Germany. Alone and aching. Waking up to the same dream every night of his friend lifting the gun...

He forced the image back. He knew it was coming—the moment when he had to deal with it, with Ronnie's mom and sister. He knew he wouldn't be able to move forward until he talked to them, but he needed some time with Ally first. Just a week.

Definitely not tonight. This wasn't the time to think about Rowe. It was time to concentrate on Ally. He wanted Ally so badly he could already taste her, but he had to prep her first. He had to whip her up into a sweet froth. Careful handling. He'd always known she would require that.

He'd spent most of his life prepping for a career as a soldier. He'd never intended to leave the military. But if he hadn't he would never have discovered this unexpected side of himself. He'd never have found out that he loved making something sweet. He adored the careful art of molding something with his hands.

He was going to enjoy using them to show Ally Jones how they could be enough for each other.

She opened the top drawer of her dresser and pulled out a long blue and green scarf.

"I'm going to cover your eyes. I want you to concentrate on one thing and one thing only. Me. My touch, my voice, what I do to you. Before I do that, I want you to take your clothes off. I want you to watch me while you do it. Watch my eyes, the way I breathe, the way this damn cock of mine will tighten. See how much you affect me."

She stood there for a moment and then her eyes came up, watching him as her hands moved to the edge of her shirt. She slowly dragged it over her head, revealing creamy skin he wanted to touch. She was wearing a plain white bra that seemed more erotic than all the Victoria's Secret specials Elise had ever worn. He didn't have a lot of experience, but he didn't need much to tell him Ally was special. She made him feel.

"Now the jeans." He wanted it to last.

She put her hands on her hips. "I've waited weeks to see that chest, Miles. I'll drop trou and everything if I get a glimpse of what's hiding under there."

Even her brat called to him. He tugged his shirt off, infinitely pleased that he'd started up a hardcore workout regime again. He hadn't liked the fact that Adam and Jake had been so much stronger. It spurred him to work harder. He might not have a right leg, but he had a cut torso.

She stared, those blue eyes wide as she took him in. It was enough to make a man feel good.

"I believe you said something about dropping those jeans." His confidence was way up just from her jaw dropping. He meant to give her the same because she was gorgeous. Inside and out.

Her hands went to the waistband of her pants. She undid the button and shoved the jeans down over her hips and to the floor.

"You know that's not all I want. I adore your every curve, but I want to see you."

He could see the way his tone worked on her. An authoritative but loving top would help her. She could work with him to bring them both great joy.

Her arms moved toward her back and in a single twist of her hand, the bra came off and her breasts sprang free. Gorgeous and round, with pretty pink and brown tipped nipples. Those breasts were breathtaking and his whole body responded. Every muscle tightened and his blood started to thrum in anticipation.

"I want more."

One elegant brow arched over her blue eyes. "So do I."

"It's not pretty, baby." But it was him. He'd come to accept it. He'd lost his leg. He'd given it for his country. At first it had seemed like nothing more than a random thing, but he'd come to believe it was a sacrifice and one willingly made if the people he loved were safe. For so long the Army had been a career and then a road that led to something new and different. He'd made his sacrifice, done his duty, and now he wanted peace and freedom and god, he wanted her.

"Says you."

He shoved his jeans down, careful around his prosthetic. It had a vacuum seal he would have to break later, but he left it on now. She should see what she was getting. He walked because of an artificial leg with a mechanized knee. He wouldn't be normal again, but he'd discovered normal was a lie. There was no such thing.

"Can I touch you?" Her hand was already up, but she didn't make a move toward him.

He wanted to get rid of this hesitancy between them. He reached out and took her hand, bringing it to his chest. "You can touch me anywhere you want."

Her fingers brushed against his skin, a light caress that left him wanting more. He stood still, giving her a chance to explore. She seemed fascinated with the hair on his chest, petting him like he was some kind of exotic beast. She traced the lines and contours of his body, moving over his muscles and smoothing across his scars. He had plenty of them.

Her fingers trailed down to his abs, running over them to the waistband of his boxers. Her eyes were staring down at his prosthetic.

"Does it hurt?"

"It can't hurt, baby." It wasn't there. He didn't want to go into the fact that it ached from time to time and that he woke trying to move a limb that was no longer there. He would probably feel it for the rest of his life, but he was trying really hard to move on without it. He wasn't sure he would be able to if she rejected him. Somehow, Ally Jones had become necessary. The leg was freaky. It could completely turn her off.

"You should never wear clothes at all, Miles. It's not pretty? That's the most ridiculous thing I ever heard. You're a freaking Greek god."

Well, at least she was accepting. He might not believe it completely, but he would take it. There had been a moment for him when he'd worried she would see all the perfect bodies on display at the play party and realize she could have someone whole. He had to make sure she understood that no one would take her pleasure and her happiness as seriously as he did.

He held up the scarf. "I'm going to blindfold you. I want you to block out everything but the sound of my voice and the touch of my hands. Can you do that?"

"I can try, but you should know that I'm not very sexual. I don't do that screaming thing other women do. Maybe it's psychological, maybe there's something physically wrong with me. I don't know, but I don't want you to expect too much."

That sounded like a challenge. He wasn't a man to turn one down.

* * * *

The minute he guided the silk around her eyes, her perspective changed. The world didn't go completely dark. There was still a bit of light, but it was inconsequential. She was dependent on him. That was the point of this exercise. She was utterly dependent on him and all she was wearing was a pair of white cotton undies.

Without the advantage of sight, her focus shifted. She was forced to acknowledge the way cool air felt against her skin, how her nipples tightened and how warm she'd become low in her pelvis.

"Tell me about your foster mother." Big hands cupped her shoulders, spreading heat where they touched. He moved them very slowly down her arms.

"I thought I was supposed to be concentrating on you."

"Yes, on following my instructions. You've evaded all my questions for a week."

She wanted to throw that back in his face. He'd evaded her for almost a year. Of course in order to do that she would have to tell him who she was and she'd almost decided that he never needed to know. Some things were better left alone. "I loved her. She didn't always know how to handle me though. She had a son. He got me."

His hands stopped moving and he brushed her hair off her back, exposing her neck. "Did you love him?"

"Oh yes." That was an easy question to answer, but she didn't want him to get the wrong idea. "He became my brother. We survived high school together."

"What happened to your family, Allyson?" The words rumbled along her nape, making her shiver even as his fingertips brushed the sides of her torso down to her hips. He was behind her, touching her gently, but there was no doubt she wasn't alone. "I'm assuming it was bad otherwise you wouldn't have been living in your car."

She stiffened, all the intimacy fleeing because she either had to lie to him or obscure the truth so that he wouldn't question her. She was trusting him with her body, her heart, but holding back the truth might be the only way to keep them together. "My brother died in an accident a year ago and I recently lost my mother to cancer. There wasn't much money and what was left went to paying hospital bills. So I packed up and came to Texas to find something new."

To find you. And I did and now I can't imagine what I would do without you.

"I'm so sorry about that, baby, but I'm glad you told me." He kissed the back of her neck and she started to relax again. "Why do you think you aren't good at sex? Look at how these pretty things respond to me."

He cupped her breasts and her nipples immediately flared to life. They tightened again, almost painfully, as if they would explode if he didn't touch them, tease them.

"They don't usually do that." She had to bite her lip to keep from crying out when he gently rolled the nubs between his thumbs and forefingers. She felt an answering pull low in her pelvis.

She could feel the heat of his mouth next to her ear. "Why? What's sex been like? Any long-term boyfriends?"

She shook her head and tried to stay still. Not being able to see him, she had to focus on the dark chocolate sound of his voice. It was so deep and melodic. "No one for the last year. I saw someone in high school and then he went to college. I stayed at home. I dated a man I met at work for a while. We saw each other off and on up until…" Ronnie died. She couldn't say that. "Mom got sick. There wasn't time for relationships."

His hand moved lower, trailing down her abdomen. He moved close to her until she could feel him against her backside. There it was, the long, hard piece of him that proved he definitely was attracted to her. Macon was built on large lines and his cock didn't seem to be the exception.

His fingers slid under the waistband of her undies. "And none of those men made you scream?"

God, she hoped she didn't disappoint him. "No. But I'll be honest, this particular episode has probably already lasted longer than my other experiences."

His mouth moved across her shoulder, dropping kisses that sweetly singed her. "You won't get that with me. I've wanted this for a very long time. Sex with my ex-wife was quick, too. She didn't like to mess up her hair and I didn't really know what I wanted." Those fingers delved deeper, getting closer and closer to her core. "I do now."

"What do you want, Macon?"

"I want a lover. Not someone who indulges me because she thinks that's what she's required to do in a relationship. I want a woman who craves me with her heart and soul because I'm the only one who can make her wet and ready simply by looking at her. It doesn't take a ton of experience to know that a woman needs time and patience to achieve her maximum potential, but it's more than simply giving to you. I want to sink into you, to know your body better than I know my own. I want to spend hours kissing every inch of you. And I want you to trust me enough to let me take control."

"That's going to be hard for me." Although it did seem to be working. Her body was primed in a way it never had been before. "But I think we can do the sex part now. I think I'm ready."

His hands came out and he took a step back. She was left standing there alone and blind. "You're not ready until I say you're ready."

He was in control. Yeah, she got that. "Sorry."

"I don't buy that for a second, but when I'm done you'll understand the difference between being wet enough for sex and being ready to make love. If all you want is another man on top of you, you should find someone else."

"I don't want that. I want you. Don't push me away. I'm trying this for the first time. You have no idea how hard I'm trying." Her instincts told her to protect herself, that this would all go bad in the end and if she made herself truly vulnerable to him he would tear her apart. But she stood there. She didn't tear the scarf off, didn't tell him to go to hell. She wanted him more than she wanted to be safe.

"Hey, I'm sorry." He was in front of her now, his big body brushing against hers as his mouth hovered right over her lips. "I've got triggers, too, baby. Please don't tell me to hurry up and get it over with. I meant what I said before. I want more this time. I can't settle for getting off. I need to mean something to you. I need the sex to be meaningful."

"It already means more to me than you can know. I'll stop pushing. Please don't stop touching me."

He kissed her, his mouth more demanding than before. His hands found her hips, dragging her into the heat of his body. She found herself deliciously crushed against him as his mouth mated with hers.

He finally moved away. "I'm going to take you to the bed now."

She was ready for him to take her hand and lead her back, but she gasped as he hooked an arm under her legs and she was pulled up into the air. There was a moment of fear because she couldn't see and she was utterly dependent on him, but this was Macon. She relaxed and let him carry her.

"I will try my hardest not to trip, baby," he said with a chuckle.

It was good to hear him laugh after all the seriousness of before. Even if he did trip, this was the type of man who would do everything he could to take the pain for himself. He would kill himself to make sure she didn't get hurt.

He was also the type of man who would be so hurt if he ever found out why she'd come here. Given everything that had happened to him, he wouldn't trust easily.

She needed time with him, needed for him to become so comfortable with her, he wouldn't walk away. She only needed a few weeks. A month, perhaps. Maybe after she married him.

God, she was in love with Macon Miles and she wanted to marry him.

He settled her on top of the covers. Like everything she'd been given since she'd met this man, the bed was lush and comfortable. Her life had become easy in a way it never had been before. Even with her mom and Ronnie, she'd had the judgment of the rest of her town. The legacy of her father's violence had been a cloud that clung to her. But here in Dallas, there was only sunshine and friendship and him.

She let him move her arms over her head.

"I want you to hold them there until I tell you it's all right to move," he commanded, his voice turning deep.

She relaxed, luxuriating in the feel of softness at her back. Her skin was sensitized, as though her pores had opened up to soak in the feeling.

"I think you're beautiful, Ally. I especially think you're gorgeous like this. The longer I'm with you, the less I think I can be happy being vanilla. I don't need it all the time, but I want nights where I'm in control, where you trust me enough to give over to me."

"I want that, too, Macon. But for now, I want you to touch me again."

"There you go giving orders." His hand covered her breast and she arched into his touch. He closed his fingers around one nipple, rolling it deliciously. "I'll teach you not to do that in here. In here, I'm the top."

He pinched down and Ally squealed, the pain so unexpected.

"Give it a second." His hand was on her belly, holding her in place. "Tell me you didn't feel that in your pussy, baby."

The pain had bitten into her, but he was right. It had morphed somewhere from her nipple to her pussy and now she had a melting sensation between her thighs. "That hurt."

"But you're not moving." His fingers slid over the crotch of her underwear. "And these seem curiously wet."

She was wet, wetter than she'd ever been before. It was disconcerting to realize how far gone she was. She kind of wanted him to pinch her other nipple, to see if the sensation worked the same way. It had to have been a mistake. She couldn't have liked it.

"Stop thinking about it." His fingers slid over her clit and she couldn't help but squirm. "Just let it be. Let me play with you. Anything you really can't handle, tell me and I'll stop, but give it a second. You can't know if you like it. Not until you've tried it. But I think you do. Your breathing changed. You panted for a minute and then relaxed. Like this."

He twisted the other nipple, a sharp edge of pain that became warmth and a druggy sense of satisfaction.

"Tell me, did that hurt enough to never have the sensation again?"

She could hear him moving, something rustling. Not being able to see was keeping her on edge, her body active and awake in a way it had never been before. "No. It hurt, but then it felt good."

There was a little sound, almost like a soft pop. "That was me taking off the leg. It's easier to be in bed without it. For all its high tech, it doesn't move like a normal leg here. Don't be afraid."

She snorted. "I'm not afraid of your leg, Miles, and get over the whole I'm not pretty thing. You're the sexiest thing I've ever seen, leg or no leg. That stump of yours is probably hot, too."

Was that why he really blindfolded her? Because he was insecure about the leg? She was fairly certain it was why he didn't play with the guys. He never wore shorts either.

The bed dipped and she was careful to keep her hands above her head. Her lover, it seemed, liked to be obeyed, and he got off track when he wasn't. When she really thought about it, this was about him. He got very distracted by disobedience. She would have to watch for that. She would also have to find a way to let him know how sexy he was, exactly the way he was.

"Do you know that I've really never been with anyone like you?" He eased on top of her and she was pinned to the bed. She loved the feel of his body on top of hers. "My ex-wife was excruciatingly polite. Even when she divorced me, she would never have said a thing about my stump."

Embarrassment flashed through her. "I'm sorry. I wasn't trying to be rude. I didn't come from the same kind of high society you did. I'm so sorry."

His body moved against hers, his mouth descended, and she felt his tongue on her nipple. "Baby, I didn't really come from that place, either. I was raised by elite military schools, and they weren't the kindest of parents. I did my duty, but with the singular exception of my brother Adam, I didn't find a true friend until I actually got out into the Army. I liked the men and women in my unit. They were real and they spoke their minds and I didn't have to worry about what was going on under their words. By then I'd already married Elise and I knew it was a mistake. I was more attracted to outspoken women, but I couldn't call it quits. I love your nipples. I love how tight they get for me."

He sucked one inside and she got the suspicion that this "playing" he wanted to do was akin to torture. She was wet and ready and it seemed so different this time. She was already feeling some pleasure and he wasn't even touching her down there.

"I don't know how to do anything other than speak my mind." What was he doing? Where was his hand going? Why did her whole body feel like a taut bow waiting to go off?

Something hard slid against her pelvis and even without the aid of her eyes, she nearly saw stars.

"Did you like that?" Macon asked.

"God, yes."

"I like it, too, but if I rub against you too much, I'll go off and I want to make this last."

Oh, god. That had been his cock. He'd slid his hard erection up against her and it had felt like heaven. "We could do it twice. I have complete faith in your ability to do it twice in one night."

That earned her a sharp nip from his teeth. She whimpered but couldn't move due to the massive hunk of man on top of her.

"I think I'll manage twice, but that doesn't mean you're going to get what you want when you want it." He slid down again, his mouth on her belly, tracing a slow line downward. "You'll get what you want. You'll get what you don't even know you want, but it's going to be on my time, baby."

His tongue dipped into her navel. She'd never considered her belly button to be an erotic zone, but warmth pooled there and she was restless. Anxiety made her try to squirm but it wasn't because she was afraid. Had any other man taken away her sight and pinned her down, she likely would have tried to fight her way out, but she understood why Macon was doing it. He'd forced her to focus solely on him. All other thoughts had been banished. She wasn't thinking about how long this would take or whether she'd properly shaved everything she needed to. There was no place for self-consciousness. There was only Macon's touch, his voice, his will.

"Do you want to keep these on, sweetness? I can make you come without penetration if you're not ready for that, but I don't know that once I get these off you I'll be able to hold back. Maybe we should leave them on as a barrier."

She didn't want any barriers between them. Her thinking was frenzied. He was so close and she really thought he was planning on spending time down there and not only with his cock. If Miles ate pussy the way he cooked—slowly, thoughtfully and with great attention to detail—she didn't want to miss it. She didn't want to play coy and hope he got the point. He'd pushed her here. He got to deal with it. "Please take them off. Please touch me there. God, I swear if you don't put your mouth on me, I'll die."

The bed moved again, but instead of pulling them off her, he ripped them. The sound of fabric tearing made her breath catch.

86

"You don't need those. I don't want you to wear them around me. I want you to walk around Top in your black skirt and know that I can have you at any moment. Every other man in the place will be looking, but I'm the only one who knows that I can flip your skirt up and be inside you in a second." Heat hovered over her pussy and she could feel his whiskers against the soft flesh of her thighs. He didn't have a full beard. He always shaved in the morning, but by evening his masculine face was covered in a sexy five-o'clock shadow. He pressed her thighs apart, exposing her. She couldn't see him, but she could feel the way he moved, making a place for himself between her legs.

She wanted it. She wanted his mouth on her so badly, but she was determined to play this his way. She knew what it meant to have no control. Macon was asking for it. Macon wanted to mean something, and she needed him to understand that he was rapidly becoming everything to her. "Yes. I'll do it. I'll walk around knowing I'm yours and you can have me any time you want."

"Oh, baby, you won't regret that because any time I have you, it's going to be so good for you. That's my goal. I want to make you feel good. I want you to know you can rely on me for anything you need. And I think you need this."

Warmth suffused her as his tongue dragged over her pussy.

"Oh my god." The words exploded from her mouth. Nothing had ever felt so good as his mouth on her, slowly moving over her sensitive flesh.

"Macon. Say my name. Who's eating your pussy? Who thinks this is the sweetest fucking treat he's ever had in his life?" He drew one side of her labia into his mouth, sucking gently before giving the other half the same treatment.

"Macon." She said his name like a prayer, a plea for continued possession.

He pressed her thighs apart and she wished she could see him, see his dark head bent over her, working her flesh like a starving man. His tongue pierced her, diving deep inside, and it took everything she had not to press against him, to take more. She wanted everything he could give her, but it went beyond that. He groaned against her skin, the sensation shooting through her. He needed this. She was giving him something he needed, something that made him happy.

For the first time in her life, she understood the real difference between having sex and making love. Sex was a function and there wasn't anything wrong with it, but this was so much more. This was truly creating something that didn't exist before. It was a bond and a promise between them.

She felt something hard move to the edge of her channel. His finger. He slowly started to push inside her while his tongue found the button of her clitoris and started working it. Her whole body went taut, right on the edge of something she'd never experienced before. She'd had mild orgasms, thought that was all there was. This was a bomb going off, detonating in her body. When she felt the barest edge of his teeth on her clit as he sucked at her, she went off like a rocket. She couldn't control it any more. Her body bucked. She shouted out his name and couldn't help but push herself at him, desperate for more of the sensation.

She felt something wet on her cheeks and then the bed buckled, Macon's body covering hers. The blindfold was off and she had to blink in the bright light.

Macon's gorgeous face was staring down at her. One big hand cupped her cheek, his thumb brushing away the tears she shed. "Are you all right?"

He had to stop treating her like she was made of glass and would break at any moment. "That depends. Can I move my arms? And when are you going to get inside me?"

The sweetest smile covered his face. "Yes and as soon as I can get a condom on."

But she'd heard her yes and that was all she needed. She brought her hands up and smoothed them over the muscles of his shoulders and down to his chiseled chest and the dusting of masculine hair she found there. Many men waxed or shaved, but Macon had just enough hair to be manly. She let her hands roam as her body was processing the delicious sensation of having exploded. She could sense how wet and messy she'd gotten, but she had the feeling Macon loved that so she wasn't about to protest. His hips were moving, cock nestled against her clit, and every time he slid it over her she shivered with the promise.

She let her hands slide down to cup his backside. God, he was muscled everywhere.

With a deep groan, he pushed himself off her and she noticed he'd placed a small stack of condoms on the bed next to them. He grinned. "Kai slipped me some as we walked out the door."

She watched him rip one open, but then her eyes slid to the most gorgeous sight she'd ever seen. He was up on one knee, his abs tight, holding the balance. He stopped in the middle of pulling the condom out and his eyes turned wary.

"Don't you fucking dare, Miles." She wasn't having a second of that. "I'm the first woman who's seen you naked since the accident, right?"

He nodded.

"Okay, then I'm the expert. Get over it. You're gorgeous and if you knew the things I was thinking about doing with that stump right now, you would blush and think I was the worst kind of pervert in the world. I'm crazy about every inch of you."

"I think I like you perverted, Allyson." He fished the condom out and started to roll it over his enormous erection.

He moved again, angling his body down, and she was made aware of the strength it took for him to get through a day. He'd been forced to relearn everything about the way he moved.

"I think I could love you, Miles." The minute the words were out of her mouth, she wanted to call them back. She'd never said those words to any man. Not one. She hadn't even said them to Ronnie and he'd been her brother. What was she thinking?

He settled on top of her. "I'm glad because I know I could love you, Jones. Give us some time, baby. We're going to be so good together."

His face went tight as he pushed against her, slowly inching his way in. Despite the fact that she was wetter than she'd been her whole life, she could feel him stretching her. He was so big, so gloriously male, and for the first time she could see the beauty in that. She'd lived in fear much of her life, but Macon's strength wouldn't be used against her. He would protect her, guard and cherish her. Even now, when he'd given her more pleasure than she'd known was possible, he was taking his time so he didn't hurt her.

She could have told him that he could do his worst. Her whole body felt languid and relaxed and she wanted to give back to him.

She could have told him that, but then he flexed inside her and the tension started to build again. He pressed in, filling her up, and she gasped at the sensation. Surely she couldn't do that again. Except it really looked like she could.

"What? Did you think I would let you get away with just one?"

Macon asked in a sexy growl. He flexed again, pushing his cock deep inside her. "I want it all, Ally. I want everything you can give me and you can definitely give me one more orgasm before I come."

He ground against her and set a hard rhythm. She angled up, trying to take him even deeper. This was what she'd been missing her whole life, this connection, this intimacy. She'd never felt as close to another human being as she did with Macon inside her, working over her, giving her everything he could. She wrapped her legs around him, circled him with her arms and sighed when he leaned down to kiss her. His mouth took hers even as he thrust in and pulled back out with his dick. His tongue found the rhythm, too.

Over and over he thrust inside until she was crying and begging for him to send her over the edge. She loved the arrogant grin he got on his face as he gave her what she wanted and she went flying all over again.

He seemed to finally lose his control as she tightened around him. When she dug her nails in, he groaned and pounded into her. Every stroke of his cock took her higher and higher until she screamed out his name and gave him everything he'd asked for.

His whole body stiffened and he held himself hard against her core.

He finally dropped down, his body sagging against hers. His head found the curve of her neck and he rested there.

She stroked his back and for once the world seemed like a peaceful place.

CHAPTER SIX

Macon smiled as his brother walked in after a brief knock on the front door. He'd left it open to get some fresh air and sunshine. He was a fresh air and sunshine kind of guy today. He was also a breakfast kind of guy. Hungry. Lots and lots of sex had made him hungry. He continued to whip the batter he was making to get it fluffy and light. "Good morning. You want a waffle? It's a waffle kind of day."

Adam was still wearing pajama pants at ten in the morning. His brother was barefoot, his dark hair wet as though he'd gotten out of the shower, dressed, and walked over. "I'm glad to hear it. I take it things went well with Ally after last night?"

Something was up, but Macon couldn't quite bring himself to get worried. His body was still humming from sex the night before…and then again this morning…and in the shower a few minutes before. Ally had finally shooed him away claiming she wouldn't be able to walk if he didn't stop.

He felt like an unruly teenager. His cock wouldn't stop. She was everything he wanted. Affectionate, giving, submissive in bed. He didn't want her submissive out of it. He liked the fact that she had her own opinions and didn't mind giving them to him. He even liked her a little bossy. He was man enough to admit that he needed it from time to time. Like her yelling at him for getting insecure about his damn leg. She liked his leg the way it was and she'd proved it by riding the damn thing to orgasm while he sucked and played with her nipples—two of the many things he found endlessly fascinating about her.

His leg was practically a sex toy. How could he hate that?

"Things are going great." Finally. It had only taken him thirty years, but his life finally felt right. He loved his job, loved living close to his brother, and now he had Ally. Whatever had brought his brother across the lawn, he was going to handle. "What's going on? You didn't walk over here to ask about my love life."

Adam leaned on the bar. "No, although Serena was planning on it. You're lucky I caught her. She was trying to sneak over before nine this morning with a plate full of muffins."

"Did she make them herself?" He loved his sister-in-law, but she wasn't the world's greatest cook. She tended to burn things or leave out key ingredients like sugar or flour. She got distracted by what she called "plot bunnies."

"Yep. That's how curious she was. And that's another reason you should thank me. You didn't have to pretend to like them." Adam threw a glance back toward the bedrooms. "So, we didn't manage to terrify her? Serena said Ally had a talk with Kai after the party was over."

"Yes, Kai is a sneaky fucker, but he means well."

"He told me you're going up to the VA with him a couple of times a month."

Macon hadn't mentioned it to Adam. He wasn't sure how good he'd be at it. He'd gone three times and it seemed to be working all right. He knew he got something out of it. "I'm just there to talk to what I like to call the 'recently relieved of limb.'"

He talked to them, gave them advice on what he'd found worked. From skin issues to keeping the muscle he had remaining on his impaired leg, he could talk about the problems they faced all day. But sometimes, they simply needed to talk, and talking to someone who understood helped.

And he'd found it helped him in immeasurable ways.

"Do you have any idea how proud I am of you, Macon? How proud she would be?" Adam's hand patted the cookbook their mother had left behind. Adam had looked through it a few times, but he'd left it with Macon.

If he didn't watch it, his brother was going to make him look like a crazy person, crying over his waffles. "I don't know. I think I gave up the right when I treated you the way I did. I think she would have been extremely disappointed in me then."

"I think if she'd lived we wouldn't have ended up the way we did. I wonder about it a lot. I think the old man loved her. There's not really another explanation. He had all the money. He had the connections. I think he loved her and the only good part of him died when she did. He got cold after that. He turned away from everything, including us. He married, but someone who had nothing in common with Mom. If Mom had lived, we would have been a family, not three males being raised to honor a name that really means nothing without some love behind it. You're going to hate me for saying this, but sometimes I'm glad you had to come here."

Macon understood. Adam wasn't saying he was happy he'd gotten injured, but it had led to a good thing. "I cursed it for so long, but I know what you mean. If it hadn't happened, we wouldn't be brothers again. I wouldn't have a family. Sometimes it's too easy to curse the place we're at in life because we can't see where the road is going to lead us. I wouldn't have found Ally."

Adam's smile put him at ease again. "I'm glad she's making you happy. She seems like a great woman. She's good with Tristan and she's become Serena's white board buddy lately. I've heard them plotting sex and murder three times this week. By the way, if you see either woman playing around with a chainsaw, hide. They're really creative."

He hadn't realized how the simple act of connecting with his brother could change his life, his perspective, his everything. Having Adam as a brother fundamentally made his life better. "I promise. And have I said thank you lately?"

"There's no need. Not ever. You're my brother and you always have a place here." Adam sobered. "I came over here to talk to you about family actually. Our very fucked up one. I got a call from Dad about twenty minutes ago."

Macon set down the whisk and felt his shoulders tighten. "What's wrong? Did he take a turn?"

Adam shook his head. "No. He's still in remission. You know I think the old goat will likely outlast the rest of us. He was looking for you. He said he doesn't have your new cell number."

"Why? He said everything he needed to say when I tried to come home." He relaxed a little. It didn't matter. What mattered was Ally and she was getting ready for breakfast and then they would go down and help out with the cleanup at Top.

"It seems that Elise has had a change of heart. She left Alan three days ago and dear old Dad thinks she's on her way down here."

Warmth spread through his system. This was what revenge felt like. Big Tag talked about it a lot. Now he got it. "Oh, she figured out Alan went through his trust fund years ago. This is a good day."

Now he could go back to his waffles. He started to warm up the iron and opened the fridge to grab the blueberries for his compote.

"He asked about you. About how you're doing with the leg," Adam said.

Macon shrugged. "He didn't care before. I'm not sure why he does now."

"I know why he cares. A private investigator called asking him about the incident that cost you your leg."

And just like that his appetite was blown. "That was a year ago."

"The PI thinks there's something you're covering up," Adam explained. "Apparently he got information from Private First Class Rowe's family. They don't believe that things went down the way you said they did."

"I told the Army everything."

Adam's voice went soft. "Macon, you were trapped underneath that car for two days."

That was only supposed to be in the official, classified report. "How do you know that?"

Adam's eyes rolled. "Do you know who I am? Do you think I can't get hold of a couple of non-sanitized reports? Hell, I didn't even have to hack anything. Big Tag got them for me. I read them on my way to pick you up."

Macon's chest felt too tight. Adam had known all along. "You read them months ago and you're only now asking about it?"

Adam shook his head. "It didn't matter before. Now it does. Now it looks like some PI is going to come after you. I need to know if you lied on that report, Macon. I need to know what happened so I can clean it up for you."

"There is nothing to clean up. We got hit by an IED and then attacked by a small group of insurgents. They took apart my whole team and I was the only one left alive. We were so deep in enemy territory that

94

I wasn't extracted for days. I was the only survivor. Why would I lie?" Because the truth would be too painful for everyone, including himself. Because Rowe deserved better than what happened to him out in that desert.

"They did a good job on the reports. They pushed them through very quickly. Someone was watching out for you, but I wish they'd fudged that one bullet. The bullet that killed Private First Class Rowe wasn't the same as the rest of your unit. They were killed with AK-47s, typical of the Taliban. Rowe was killed with a nine-millimeter handgun."

"Don't push me Adam." He wasn't ready for this. Not even close.

"You need to talk to his mother."

"I know." He needed to face the mother and the sister. What was her name? Sarah. Carla and Sarah Rowe. He would explain everything to them. Everything except the truth. They didn't need to know that. Maybe once he talked about how brave Ronnie was, how much he'd liked the man, maybe they would back off. As for the investigator, he didn't even know how to handle that.

"You know what Dad thinks, right?" Adam stared at him, the ugly truth sitting between them.

He nodded. It was one more reason for his father to hate him.

"You know I understand," Adam said, sympathy plain on his face. "I know why you're being quiet. You have to tell them. You have to tell that family why you lied. No one who understands what it's really like out there would think twice about doing what you did. It's exactly the reason they pushed that report through as fast as they did. Everyone knows what really happened and why you would lie about it."

"Rowe's mother and sister don't know and I can't tell them, Adam. I can't fucking tell them the truth." At least his brother didn't think the worst of him.

A long sigh came from Adam as he obviously decided to give up the fight. For now. "All right. I'm going to put Ian on the investigator. He'll get it all shut down and I'll look into the family. I'll see what I can do, but I still think you should talk to them."

"Find out if they're okay." Guilt sat in his gut. He should have talked to them before now, but he'd been so lost. He knew beyond a shadow of a doubt that he couldn't really move on with Ally until he'd dealt with the Rowes. "Find out about them. I know he was born in Alabama, but I think his family moved all up and down the Gulf."

"I'll get started on it tomorrow."

"Or maybe I should reply to his sister's e-mail." She hadn't written him for weeks now, but he could find the address.

Adam shook his head. "You could have done that in the beginning, but not now. They've complicated the situation by bringing in private detectives. Let me handle this part. Let me and Jake figure out exactly what their situation is. I think it's best if you go in knowing what to expect."

"Let me know what you find out."

The door opened and Ally walked out, her hair in a towel. Her body was wrapped in a robe and she gave Adam a smile as she headed straight for the coffee. There was something so right about having Ally walk through the house in a robe. Like she belonged here with him. "Good morning, Adam."

"Morning, Ally. I'll talk to you two later." His brother pushed off from the bar. "And I'll get back to you by Wednesday, Macon."

Ally looked at him over her coffee mug. "Get back to you about what?"

The screen swung shut and Macon tried to let the tension leave with him. He didn't want Ally looking into this. She could be very bossy if she thought there was a problem. He needed to get his ducks in a row and then he would sit her down and explain what he'd done and why he needed to ensure Ronnie's family never knew. She would see that he was right and help him. He knew it. She was the one. "Just some business we're dealing with. Come here. I need you to stir while I get the griddle ready. I think Sunday waffles are a new tradition."

Her arms came around his back and flattened against his chest. She pressed herself against him and he was glad he'd left off the shirt. He'd put on a pair of shorts for the first time in forever. He was actually comfortable for once and all because Ally had convinced him he wasn't a freak. Well, he kind of was, but that was a good thing.

He felt her kiss his back. "I like the sound of that, Miles."

She kissed him again and then got down to serious whisking.

He worked beside her, listening to her hum.

It was going to be all right. For the first time since the accident, he had real hope for the future.

* * * *

Three days later, Ally wiped down the last of the new tables and breathed deeply. Chef was breaking in some of the new appliances. She could smell the heavenly scent of braised short ribs. The kitchen doors opened and she got the briefest glimpse of her hunky guy. He was leaning over his station, patiently decorating the strawberry Napoleons he was testing out tonight.

"Okay, what if her partner somehow managed to get the information uploaded to her GPS before he was murdered. Then she's got the location of the reports in her navigation system and all she has to do is follow instructions," Serena said as she walked back from where she'd been hanging new drapes.

Serena had been combating writer's block for days. She claimed doing tasks like cleaning or decorating helped get her head back in the game.

"Does a GPS work like that?" Deena asked.

Serena shrugged. "It could be a new GPS."

"So the GPS takes over and sends her to someplace she wasn't expecting? That sounds more like a horror novel to me. This is why you can keep your fancy cars. Bessie never talks back and she doesn't tell me where to go." Ally was wary of some satellite telling her what the roads were like. She'd driven all the way from small-town Georgia to Dallas without the aid of some robo voice telling her where to go. Of course, she'd also made a wrong turn in Louisiana and was almost certain she'd nearly been murdered by cannibalistic bayou dwellers, but she'd made it out of that, too.

"I don't know. I kind of like it," Deena said, sitting down next to Serena.

They started talking about plots, but Ally's head wasn't in the game. She'd gotten herself into trouble again and there wasn't a road map out of this one.

How long could she go without telling Macon the truth? She was in love with the man. One hundred percent, fallen in crazy, no going back love. He was the man for her and she knew deep down that whatever he was hiding about Ronnie's death couldn't be so bad. Macon was honorable.

Of course, he also claimed he was a changed man. He talked about the fact that he'd been different before. She hadn't known that Macon.

She glanced down at her watch. They were T-minus forty-five minutes to dinner service. Of course it was family dinner service, as Chef Taggart liked to call it. He was prepping dinner to thank all his friends and family who had come in this week to get Top back into shape for the upcoming weekend. They'd only been forced to close for two weeks thanks to the Herculean efforts of staff and Taggart's friends. Big Tag had been in most afternoons with a tool kit and at least one baby strapped to his chest. It had been kind of fun. They'd set up playpens and the kids had gnawed on wooden blocks or each other while the adults worked.

She'd fit in. Ever since that night at the play party, Macon's relatives had treated her like one of their own. She was closest to Serena, but she was getting to know Grace and Charlotte and Avery. She and Avery were trying to teach Eve McKay how to knit. The gorgeous psychologist knew how to curse, but she was trying to be patient.

What would they think of her if they knew she was lying?

"Hello?" A soft feminine voice brought Ally out of her thoughts. She looked up and a stunning blonde stood in the lobby. She was tall and willowy, like she'd stepped out of the pages of a fashion magazine. Dressed in a yellow sundress that had to be designer, she glanced around Top curiously.

Serena and Deena were deeply engrossed in a discussion of whether or not the GPS could easily be hacked via cell phone, so Ally stood up. "I'm sorry. We're not actually open to the public until Friday."

The woman laughed. "Oh, I'm not here for dinner. I'm sure it's a fine establishment and all, but no. I'm looking for my husband. I've been told he works here."

Who among the guys was married? Most of the line chefs were single. "What's your husband's name? I'll go in the back and get him."

Somehow, she couldn't imagine any of the rough-and-tumble guys who worked here being married to the supermodel. She was the graceful type who screamed money and good breeding. She wasn't the type who married dudes who ended up in the military unless they were officers.

"Macon Miles," she said with a smile.

"Holy shit." Serena was suddenly at her side. "Are you Elise?"

Elise Miles. Macon's ex-wife was standing right here in the middle of Top looking like an angel. Every hair was perfectly placed, her makeup artful but not overdone. She was wearing a pair of five-inch heels that would have caused Ally to break her neck, but naturally Elise

Miles walked perfectly in them. She kind of floated across the tile.

She held out a manicured hand. "Why, yes, I am. I see Macon's talked about me."

"Only using four letter words," Ally said with a frown.

Serena elbowed her. "I've seen a picture. My husband had a picture from your wedding. I believe Macon sent it to him back before Adam was cut off from the family."

"Yes, I'd heard Adam had married. It's so good that he finally realized he could be normal," Elise said.

Jake chose that moment to step out of the men's room where he'd been fixing a leaky sink. He walked right up to Serena and planted a kiss on her cheek. "I'm going to grab a beer, baby. Tell Adam I'm out back when he gets here with Tristan."

Serena smiled. "Jake, don't you want to meet Elise?"

He shrugged. "Sure, who's Elise?" He turned to the newcomer and his eyes went wide. "Holy shit."

"That's what I said. She's happy Adam's finally normal," Serena said under her breath.

That brought a snort from Jacob Dean. "Yeah, we're the most normal threesome here. I'm going to go make a phone call. Nice to meet you. Looking forward to the drama."

Jake practically ran into the kitchen.

"Well, is someone going to get my husband? I need to speak with him." Elise's shoe tapped impatiently.

"Ex."

"Excuse me?"

"You're divorced. Macon is your ex-husband." Ally couldn't stand the way the beauty queen possessively called Macon her husband. "The last he heard, you were busy getting ready to marry his brother."

The angel's eyes turned cold and narrowed as she looked down at Ally. "That was a mistake and absolutely none of your business. Look, I can tell from your sad waitress eyes that you have a thing for my husband, and maybe he's even given you hope that you can be with him, but I'm telling you to step aside. This isn't going to go your way. That man has been mine since we weren't even old enough to drink. I get that I hurt him and he's been slumming, but I assure you, he'll go home with me." She looked up and a glorious smile crossed her lips. "Hey, babe. You look good."

Ally turned and there was Macon looking all hot and masculine in his chef's whites and khaki slacks. He stood in the doorway, a hand on his hip. "You look here. Why are you here, Elise?"

At least he wasn't melting at the sight of her. He was frowning, but he looked more confused than angry. He didn't look at Ally at all. There was no welcoming smile on his lips, nothing at all that would calm her down. He only had eyes for his ex.

"I need to talk to you." Elise's eyes picked up the light and there was no way to miss the shimmer of tears there. "It's been a long time."

Macon kept frowning, but he nodded toward a table in the back. "All right. Come on."

Elise's heels didn't even clack across the floor. It was like the woman didn't weigh a thing. No pair of her shoes would ever be so gauche as to thud or squeak when she wasn't actively trying to make the sound. Oh, no. Not Princess Elise.

Serena put a hand on her arm. "It's all right. He's only going to talk to her."

Ally hoped she looked absolutely nothing like she felt. She felt like picking up a chair and bashing it over Princess Elise's blonde head. Instead, she simply shrugged. "Of course."

She noticed Jake and Big Tag walking out of the kitchen. They each had a beer in hand and each man was carrying a tiny infant girl. It looked like Charlotte was still out shopping. They sat at a table across the room from Macon and his former bride, but they didn't even try to hide their curiosity.

"Kala, this is what's called drama. This is what we live for, baby girl." Ian tipped his beer back. "Way better than TV."

Jake frowned and looked down at his identically dressed infant. "How do you know which one is which?"

"A father always knows," Big Tag said. "Also, I marked this one with a Sharpie. See, it looks like a tiny mole right behind her ear. That's Kala."

Serena gasped. "Ian Taggart, that's horrible."

He shrugged. "Nah, what's horrible is I'm trying to figure out a way to make it permanent. Is it illegal to tattoo a baby?"

"Yes," Serena and Ally managed to say at the same time.

Big Tag shook his head. "It's nothing. It's not like I'm putting a skull and crossbones on her. It's a miniscule dot so neither one of these girls can pull one over on the old man." He pointed to the baby in Jake's arms. "Yeah, I'm looking at you, Kenz. I see how you roll over and try to pretend to be Kala. I'm not blind. Daddy sees everything. Including how you look at that Tristan kid. Stay away from him."

"Ian, she's eight weeks old," Serena pointed out. "Tristan recently turned one. I hardly think they're planning to date."

"Yeah, well, it's never too early to start. I know what your boy's going to think. He's going to think Mom didn't have to pick, why should I, and then suddenly my sweet baby girls are in some weirdo relationship where they have to worship the boy."

Jake flipped him off but smiled down at Kenzie. "Don't listen to your father. Tristan's going to be a gentleman. Ooo, what do you think she said?"

Macon's hands were in fists on the table, his back ramrod straight. Finally he was showing a little anger. She could deal with anger.

"It's all right," Serena said, giving her a half hug as they watched the table. "He's going to tell her to go any minute now and then everything will be right back to normal."

"I have to be reasonable." Ally said the words as though saying them would calm her. They didn't really.

"Oh, what's the fun in that?" Big Tag asked.

"Ignore him. He lives for this kind of thing," Serena said, glaring at the big guy. "There's absolutely no reason to get upset. He didn't invite her here."

"But he knew she was probably on her way," Jake said.

"What?" That was completely news to her.

Jake winced, like he knew he'd screwed up. "Sorry. Uhm, Adam told him on Sunday that it was a distinct possibility, but I don't think Macon really gave a damn."

He'd known for days that his ex-wife might show up and he hadn't mentioned it? Was he happy to see her? Was the whole angry thing only for show? Maybe he wanted to have the upper hand. Elise was right. They had been together for most of their adult life, though Macon had been in combat for a good portion of their marriage. Did he want to give it another shot?

"He certainly doesn't care about her anymore," Jake said quickly. "I'm sure of that."

"Well, it sure looks like she cares about him," Big Tag said. He bounced his daughter gently as she gurgled up at him and tugged on his shirt. "That, baby girl, is what we guys call manipulation. You see when a woman wants a man to do something, sometimes she strokes his hand like she's stroking another part of his anatomy he really wants stroked. She often doesn't really go through with this, but some guys are dumbasses."

Sure enough, Elise had a hand on Macon's arms, stroking from his elbow down to the wrist. She held his hand in hers and the free hand kept stroking as she spoke. Even from where Ally stood she could see the crocodile tears clinging beautifully to Elise's high cheekbones.

"Still, reason and rationality will win the day," Serena said.

Her hands were shaking with anger. What right did that woman have to come in here and try to take her man? Macon was hers. He damn straight better be because she was the one he humped like fifteen times a day. She'd been worried she was going to walk funny after his crazy "try it" play session the night before. Had Elise been the one who let him play with a butt plug? Nope. That had been her. Had Elise let him tie her up and torture her with his tongue for what had to be an hour? Definitely not.

But Serena was right. She had to be calm. "I will talk to him about it after she leaves. Then we can sit down and have a good chat about why she came here."

"Oh, I think she came here to try to sleep with your man, Jones," Big Tag said.

"Stop," Jake nagged.

"Come on. Tell me you don't want to see what happens when her inner redneck makes an appearance. Ain't no redneck like a Georgia redneck. Her accent's already gotten deeper. Look at the way her hands have that slight shake to them. She's thinking about killing Miss New York," Taggart explained. "I'm going to lay a hundred on Georgia there."

Jake shook his head. "I'd be stupid to take that bet. Ally could take that plastic Barbie doll down in a heartbeat."

"She's not going to because she doesn't have to," Serena insisted. "She's the lady in this scenario and she's very secure in her relationship."

Nope. She really wasn't. Macon was gorgeous and well educated and he'd come from money. Oh, he might not have a lot of it now, but a man like Macon wouldn't be down for too long. Wouldn't he want a sophisticated wife like Elise by his side?

Elise moved her chair to be closer to him. It didn't take a lip reader to see she was telling him she was sorry and she thought she deserved a second chance. No. They deserved a second chance. That was the way a woman like Elise would play it.

Elise reached up and brushed back his hair.

And Ally was done.

"Thank god. Go for it, Georgia," Big Tag said as she strode back over to the table.

She wasn't going for anything, but she deserved some respect. "Hi, I'm assuming Macon hasn't explained things, but I would really appreciate it if you would not touch my boyfriend in such an intimate way."

There. That was polite. That wasn't slamming a fist in her face. It was good. She was a Southern Belle. Not a crazed redneck.

Macon had turned and one brow arched over his face. "I did mention you, baby. You need to stay calm. You have nothing to be jealous over."

Elise rolled her eyes. "You should leave and let me and Macon work this out." She turned back to Macon, her hand right back over his. "Macon, I forgive you for leading that waitress person on. I understand."

"That's very mature of you," Macon replied, dragging his hand back. "You should probably stop now."

"I blame myself. I was so upset over what happened to you overseas. You lost your leg, Macon. Do you know how hard that was on me?" She reached down and touched his leg and then pulled back, distaste evident.

"Yeah, that's the one," Macon drawled.

She moved her hand to the whole leg. "I think we should give it another shot."

"I am going to shoot you if you don't get your hand off his leg. Both of them. Don't you ever touch his stump again, lady. That is mine and I will lose my shit if you put a hand on it." All of her life she'd been told she had her daddy's temper. Well, she was going to try really hard not to kill anyone, but she might be fighting a losing a battle.

Macon turned slightly, his eyes finding hers. "Baby, I really can handle this. Why don't you go and finish up the Napoleons? They need a glaze. You know how to do that."

He'd been teaching her, patiently going over every step and letting her mess up entire batches so she could learn. She was about to nod and go and finish up. When Macon used that tone, he liked to be obeyed. He didn't use it very often. For the most part, he was incredibly indulgent. He never said a word when she yelled at him to hurry up or moaned about the fact that he left his towels all over the floor. He simply picked them up and apologized and kissed her. So he wasn't the crazed-Alpha, you-must-obey-me-at-all-costs Dom. And she could be the reasonable, trusting girlfriend.

She managed to get a few steps toward the kitchen when she turned to look at Macon one last time. She trusted him. She believed in him. If he said he could handle this, then he would.

That was when Elise smirked her way. "Yes, why don't you go and finish up in the kitchen while my husband handles me. He handles me quite well."

Macon opened his mouth to say something, and that was when Elise leaned over and planted her lips on his.

"Take it." Serena pushed an umbrella her way. It had been sitting near the coat rack in the lobby, so Ally knew her friend had walked back to get it. "Time for reason is over. Kill the bitch."

Macon managed to move out of Elise's arms, but Ally had had enough. It was time to stake her claim and let the Elises of the world understand what happened when she tried to take a Georgia girl's man.

Ally held the umbrella like a baseball bat and managed to see Elise through a haze of red mist that seemed to have filtered into the room. "I told you to get your hands off him."

Elise finally seemed to give a damn. She jumped back. "Macon, tell your crazy girlfriend to lay off."

Macon stood up and sighed. "Yeah, I think we're past that now. Don't kill her, baby. Taggart, I'll take one of those beers. If she can flame out on my ex-wife, I can have a single beer."

"Feel free." Macon could have a six-pack and not scare her. They had moved past that particular trigger. He was probably a very affectionate drunk. "I will take care of this situation." She focused all her attention on the woman who'd had a hand on her man. "Get out now and don't you dare come back."

Elise took a step toward the lobby. "Macon, you need to protect me."

Macon was sitting down with Big Tag and had that long overdue beer in his hand. "I already gave a leg for my country, Elise. I'm all out of protection for anyone I'm not actively fucking. Unfortunately, you're up against the crazy lady I am screwing on a regular basis, so you're on your own. Ally, you know we're going to have a long talk after this is done, right?"

He was going to require a short period of complete obedience and she would give it to him. She brought the umbrella down on the table right in front of Elise, glorying in the way she jumped.

"The next time that's going to be your head," Ally vowed.

"You pathetic piece of trash. You can't keep him," Elise said with a snarl. She held her handbag up like it was protection. "When he wakes up he's going to realize he needs a woman with some class, someone he can be proud of."

The words cut, but she wasn't about to let that show to Elise Miles. God, she was jealous. She hated the fact that the woman still had his name. How could he have married this cold woman? Except that Elise was right and he needed someone well bred, someone who could move through society properly.

"Out," Ally yelled and she realized she had more than a small audience now. She turned slightly and saw that Chef Taggart, Eric, and the rest of the crew had come out of the kitchen and were actively watching the scene being performed in front of them.

Yeah, she was making quite the impression, but she couldn't back down now. If she was about to get fired, she was going to make sure there was a damn good reason behind it. She marched on Elise.

Those five-inch heels could really move when they wanted to. Elise hauled her skinny ass toward the front door.

"Macon!" Elise shouted, her arms out as though they could protect her. "Macon, please."

"It pleases Macon to not have anything to do with you." Macon yawned and tipped back his beer. "We're divorced. We're going to stay that way. Go back to New York. Find some other rich idiot to take care of you. The bank's closed here. I'm a working man now."

"If you would talk to your father," Elise pleaded.

Ally was done talking. She swung the umbrella, narrowly missing the blonde, but then she'd planned it that way.

Elise screamed and Taggart shouted out something about a swing and a miss.

Ally chased the lovely Elise right out onto the street. The minute she could, she locked the door. That woman wasn't getting back in.

"And stay out. You aren't welcome at Top." She turned, her hands still on the umbrella.

Big Tag and Jake clapped, but they weren't the only ones. She looked over and the entire kitchen staff plus Deena, Tiffany, and Jenni were cheering her on. Thank god.

Chef Taggart gave her a thumbs-up. "Way to take out the trash, Ally."

But Macon frowned her way. He stood as she walked back into the dining room. "Chef's office. Now."

"Back to work. We've got dinner soon. And Miles, I'll handle the glaze, but you better clean up after yourself, if you know what I mean," Chef said.

She turned again, well aware her trouble was just starting.

CHAPTER SEVEN

Macon closed the door behind him without looking over at Ally. He wasn't angry, but he needed to make a few things plain to her. She'd put herself in harm's way. She could still be there. Elise's father was a lawyer. He wouldn't be surprised if Ally didn't find herself being served papers in the next few weeks. They would deal with it, but things would have been infinitely simpler if she'd done as he'd asked her to.

The door locked with an audible snick.

"Macon, are you mad at me?" Now she managed a soft voice, her accent coming out like sweet syrup.

He crossed over to the closet where he knew damn well Sean kept some necessary items. By telling him to "clean up" after himself, Sean had been giving him permission to use his office for the very necessary disciplining of his submissive.

He was about to find out if she could really handle what he needed her to. Being with Allyson had made it clear to him this was absolutely what he wanted.

"No, but we're going to have a talk about what it means to be a couple." Ah, there it was. A nice long length of jute. He pulled it out.

Her eyes widened at the sight, but she didn't protest. "I didn't like the way she touched you. She didn't have the right to kiss you."

He unrolled the rope, getting a feel for it. "You're right. She didn't and I can't tell you how good your possessiveness makes me feel, baby. I want this to work both ways. I'm never going to like another man looking at you, much less actually laying a hand on you. Take off your clothes."

"What? I thought we were talking."

"Yes, we're going to talk with you naked."

"And the rope?"

"Naked and tied up," he clarified.

She sighed but started to work out of the T-shirt she was wearing. She dragged it over her head and folded it before unclasping the bra she really didn't need to wear. Those breasts were two of the perkiest, prettiest things he'd ever seen. It was a shame to bind them up. "I know I lost my temper, but she kissed you."

And that had driven his sweet girl absolutely insane. She'd been right. She really had lost her shit and now everyone at Top knew Macon had a girl who would defend his honor against all threats. "Now the pants. And I understand, but I could have handled it. I'm worried you've opened a nice-sized can of worms."

She folded the jeans and stood in front of him completely naked, her hands on her hips as she glared up at him. "I'm not apologizing, Macon. She touched your leg."

He couldn't help but chuckle about that. He would bet she'd been more pissed about Elise's hand on his quarter leg than she'd been about the kiss. "I understand, but it would have been better for you if you'd done as I asked. Her father is a highly litigious man. He lives for nuisance lawsuits. She's very likely on the phone with him right now."

She shrugged, tossing her hair back in her sassy way. "Bring it on. I seriously doubt she's going to find it worth her while. I don't have any money. Besides, I didn't even hit her."

He felt bad about explaining the full situation to her, but she needed to understand he hadn't given the order for his health. He'd actually loved watching her go a little crazy. She'd wielded that damn umbrella like a deadly weapon. It had been satisfying to see Elise duck and run.

"Sean didn't hit her either, but she could potentially sue Top."

The color drained from her face. "I didn't think about that."

"Yes, I realize that, but I did and that's why I requested you go into the kitchen and let me handle things. Were you worried I was going to cheat on you?"

Tears filled those perfect eyes, and it took everything he had not to scoop her up and hold her close. "No. I didn't think you would cheat. If you were going to go with her, you would have broken it off with me first. Did I really get the restaurant in trouble?"

At least she trusted him. He was still worried she'd taken Elise's words to heart. The woman had always known how to get under an opponent's skin. It was her superpower. "I don't know, but we'll handle it. There were plenty of witnesses who will likely say you behaved in an appropriate manner, but that's not the point. I won't ever put my foot down unless it's important, Allyson. We have to figure out how we'll work as a couple, but I can tell you when I finally do put that foot down, I expect to be obeyed. Did you understand what I wanted you to do?"

She sniffled, but he was pleased with how comfortable she was with her nudity. The first few times he'd required her to chuck her clothes, she'd been self-conscious, but it seemed she'd gotten the idea that he appreciated her body. "Yes. I knew what you wanted and I knew what would happen if I didn't. I knew you would need a session. I didn't know you kept rope lying around though. That was a surprise."

"Oh, baby, I don't need rope to discipline you. I can always find something. The kitchen is a veritable store of things I can use to swat your pretty rear. Put you hands together and hold them out."

She put her wrists together and held them toward him. "Are you going to spank me? I can handle it."

He'd figured her out a bit. She would always be a mystery to him. There would be small spaces inside her that weren't open to him, but he could deal with that. He'd learned she could handle some loving discipline as long as he was affectionate with her afterward. "I'm going to spank you. I think you've certainly earned twenty smacks and then you're going to take care of me. When I tell you to, you'll get on your knees and you'll suck me dry. Is that understood?"

He worked while he talked, moving the jute up and over and around, forming a pattern that would sit on her skin for a while after he'd removed the rope. It wasn't too tight, but he wanted her to sit at dinner with the marks as a visible reminder of his possession. It wasn't simply about reminding her. There was a part of him that wanted the rest of them to see he was properly topping this woman.

"Let me make something clear. I have no intentions of leaving you. Why would you think about that?"

Her eyes were on the rope, watching as he moved the pattern up.

Had she been a bustier girl, he wouldn't have been able to tie her this way, but Allyson was particularly flexible with her arms. They'd played with ropes over the last few nights. He liked this pattern. It made her look vulnerable.

"Macon, some of the things she said were true."

"Which ones? The one about how my losing a leg was really the hardest on her? Or how running off with my brother was probably my fault because I'd left her alone while I was fighting a war?"

Her eyes flared. "Are you serious?"

"As a heart attack, baby. You weren't listening to her. I would never fall for her shit, but I've learned that unless I let her have her say she won't stop. I was going to listen and then explain in no uncertain terms that my life is here now and it's with you. She's not welcome here. I want to be right here with the right job and the right woman."

"But she's wasn't lying about me. I'm not well bred. My only family connections are currently in the Georgia penitentiary. I'm a liability to a man like you."

"That's another ten swats. And what do you mean by 'a man like me'? Bend over."

She leaned over Sean's desk, her bound arms forming a base to balance from. It would be difficult. She would have to think about not falling to one side or the other. That was exactly what he wanted. He looked down and stared at that luscious ass of hers. The cheeks were plump and perfect, and he adored the twin dimples on the small of her back.

"You won't always want to be a pastry chef at a small restaurant," she said. "Eventually you'll need more. You were raised to be ambitious. You came from a wealthy family."

He ran a hand over her cheeks. They'd played at light spanking, nothing serious. Even as he let his palm explore he knew he wouldn't go too hard on her. Even this was mostly play. Spanking her wouldn't correct the behavior. Knowing that she could have hurt Sean would correct the behavior. This was about allowing him to feel like he was in control and he was deeply grateful to have found a woman who understood. "Let me know if this scares you, baby."

He brought his hand up and then down with a satisfying smack to the center of her backside. She gasped and then settled in.

"That's not so bad. I told you. I can handle this, Miles."

110

He slapped her ass again, harder this time. "That's two. I might come from a wealthy family but I never enjoyed the money." His hand moved, forming a pattern across the fleshy part of her ass. "Three. Four. And I wasn't raised to be ambitious. I was raised to be a soldier. It's what Miles men have done for generations. I was supposed to be a general like my father and my grandfather. Five. Six. I was supposed to marry the right woman. Seven. I was not supposed to get my leg blown to hell and get involved in potential scandals. Eight. Nine. Ten."

"Scandal?" The question came out on a breathy gasp.

He was not getting into it right now. He wanted a moment of pleasure with her, not a rundown of everything he'd done wrong. "It's not important. Eleven and twelve. The point is my life hasn't gone the way my father thought it should. Will I always want to be right here? I don't know, but I do know I'm going to want to be with you."

He got down to spanking her, relieved when he caught some sure signs that she was enjoying her discipline. When his fingers brushed against her, he could feel the way her pussy was getting wet and ripe, smell the sweet scent of her arousal. She went up on her toes with the next smack and he could see in the low light how pink her backside was becoming. When he got to twenty, he felt his cock tighten. He'd been hard since she'd walked in the room, but his erection was reaching epic proportions. His leg had been aching from standing far too long, but none of that mattered because Ally was accepting the relationship. He'd been afraid in the beginning that they wouldn't be able to get past her disdain, but she'd thrown herself into the lifestyle, trying the things he asked her to and being honest about what she did or didn't like. She could handle spanking and a light crop, but she wanted nothing to do with canes. She preferred the feel of warm flesh against hers and he liked to give her what she wanted.

"How are you doing?" He looked down and there were tears glistening in her eyes.

"I hated seeing her with you. I can't stand the thought of that woman having your name." The desolation in her voice made him stop. He quickly helped her up and had her unbound in a few seconds. She was crying freely by the time he tossed the rope aside and gathered her up. He ran his hands up and down her arms to make sure she had circulation before wrapping himself around her as she wept against his chest.

"I'm sorry, baby. She means nothing to me."

"You loved her."

Had he? "I thought I did, but marrying her was also a means to an end. My father was friends with hers. My father and stepmother thought it was a good match and I wanted to take the next step. I guess you're right. I was raised to be ambitious. I was raised to constantly move forward, to always have a goal, and part of that stage of my life was to get married."

"You were so young."

She felt right cuddled up against him. He sank down into the big chair, settling her on his lap. "I wanted to move to the next part of my life. I suppose what I really wanted was a family. I thought if I married and had some kids, maybe it would make up for feeling so alone growing up." He let his fingers tangle in her hair, holding her close. "I'm not going to want her back. I'm not going to want some aristocratic life. I want this life."

She sat up, her eyes finding his. "I want this life, too. I want it with you. Macon, I don't know what I would do without you."

She'd had so much taken from her. "You don't have to find out. I'm not going anywhere."

She put her arms around him and brushed her mouth to his. "I'm crazy about you, Miles. I promise I'll listen to you next time, but you should know that any time another woman touches you, I'll probably want to kick her ass."

"And then I'll spank yours." He kissed her again, lingering this time. "Did I hurt you?"

She shook her head. "No. I got emotional. Seeing her made me a little insecure. I needed this. I needed to be with you." She hopped off his lap and turned away from him. She placed her palms flat on the desk. "You owe me ten more."

She was presenting to him and his cock hardened painfully.

"Not like that," he said, his voice going deep. "I want you to bend over and grab your ankles."

She moved back and then gracefully bent over and found her position.

Macon stood up. This was exactly what he wanted. The position allowed her pussy to peek out, showing off glistening folds that were begging for the attention of his mouth or his cock. He settled for fingers for the moment. "This is interesting." He slid a single finger along her labia. "I was worried you would never enjoy this part of play, but your pussy seems to like it fine."

"I like it with you. I couldn't do this with anyone else."

He pressed his finger in, angling inside her as he used his free hand to swat her ass. "Now that we've discussed the situation with my ex-wife and your homicidal proclivities, let's move on to the secondary punishment."

He slowly fucked that finger in and out of her pussy. He smacked her ass again, this one a hard swat that sounded through the quiet room. "I don't ever want to hear you talk bad about yourself again. I don't like it."

Another one, exactly as rough. He could be indulgent on the first issue, but he wouldn't be disobeyed on this one. No one got to talk shit about her. Not even her.

"I promise," she vowed, her voice a breathy plea.

He gave her every spank he'd promised. All the while his finger moved in and out of her body. He teased at her clit. A bit of sugar and then a hard slap. By the time he was done, she was soaking wet and wanting so much more than he was willing to give her in that moment. "Up. Now you take care of me."

The pleading look on her face almost made him change his plans. Almost.

She dropped to her knees in front of him, her hands on the fly of his slacks. She tugged them down. Her hand ran over the skin of his thigh and he nearly growled in pleasure. He'd thought the useless piece of flesh was something he would have to try to hide if he ever took a lover, but Ally didn't pull away or avert her eyes. She slid her nails right down to where his flesh met the C-Leg. She teased him, running her fingertips across the skin and sensitizing it while her mouth got closer and closer to where he needed it to be.

He reached down and tangled a hand in her hair. She was not in control of this. "Lick me, Allyson. Lick me and take me deep or we're not done with the punishment."

She pouted beautifully, but there was a grin on her face when she leaned over and gripped his cock right before running her tongue over the head.

He bit back a groan. It wasn't only about how good it felt to have that tongue of hers coating his cock. He got hot just from the act of her submitting to him. Ally was strong, so strong, and she had emotional issues, but she pushed through because she wanted to please him. It made him willing to do anything to keep her by his side.

He was falling in love with this woman and he finally understood what the phrase really meant. His marriage to Elise had been about trying to find something, attempting to build something he'd never really had before. His relationship with Ally was as natural as breathing. It wasn't merely something to build, but something to build on. Ally was his foundation.

She sucked gently on the head and he watched as his cock started to disappear behind her lips.

Her tongue whirled all around, pure pleasure swamping his senses. She sucked on the head, her tongue sliding over the slit where pre-come pulsed out. Her eyes were up, watching him as she reached up and cupped his balls. He gritted his teeth against the need to thrust hard and fast, preferring to revel in the soft feel of her mouth, the way her hands moved on his skin.

She worked his dick into her mouth, inch by inch. Each slow pass brought him closer and closer to the soft velvet at the back of her throat.

Her tongue dragged over the underside of his cock and then rolled around lazily, tracing and exploring the lines of his erection. He allowed her to play for a moment. She gripped his cock with one soft hand, squeezing him tight while she worked his cockhead, suckling and teasing him until he couldn't take another second.

"Stop playing. I want to fuck your mouth." His hand gently gripped her hair, forcing her to still. She went compliant, allowing him to force another inch of his cock inside. It still wasn't enough. God, he couldn't get enough of her. He might never be able to get enough of her.

The silk of her hair played against his hand as he gently pulled on it. A low moan came from her throat, reverberating all over his dick. She liked it when he pulled her hair, never too much. He didn't want to hurt her, merely sensitize her to his touch. Her scalp would light up a little when he tugged on her hair. He wanted every inch of her flesh alive and pulsing with pleasure. He needed to teach her that he was the man who could make her feel. He wanted to be that man because absolutely no other woman had ever made him feel the way Ally did.

But now he wanted to concentrate on the drag of her tongue over his cock.

She relaxed and let him thrust in and out of her mouth. Every moan she made tingled along his cock and brought him closer and closer to the edge. They'd played at D/s up to this point, but he was going to move them along. He wouldn't want to squash her spirit. Her crazy, independent, gorgeous soul was the reason he loved her, but she needed someone who would watch out for her. Someone who would make sure she never lived in her car again or put herself in a position where she could get hurt. He would gently curb her self-destructive tendencies and she would bring him out of his self-imposed shell.

He looked down on her, his cock taking over. He loved her. He loved her so fucking much. He was thirty years old and had been married for over a decade, but Allyson Jones was the first woman he'd ever loved.

Another thrust brought him to the soft spot at the back of her throat. Ally swallowed around him and there was no fighting it anymore. His whole body stiffened as he came, pulsing streams into her sweet mouth.

His submissive did as she'd been asked. She took it all. Ally swallowed everything he had to give her and she did it with her eyes up, staring at him like she couldn't get enough.

He'd intended this to be punishment. He'd intended to spank her, fuck her mouth and then make her wait until after dinner to get hers.

She licked his cock one last time before sitting back. "Is Sir pleased?"

It was the smile on her face that did it. That smile wasn't a smirk or sarcasm. She was happy. She was happy to be with him, to make love with him. He'd put that smile on her face and it made him feel larger, more satisfied than anything he'd done before. With Allyson by his side, he could face what he needed to. He could move on because now he had a true partner.

"Sir is madly in love with you." He reached down and helped her stand, his mouth finding hers.

Punishment could wait. He simply wanted her.

* * * *

Ally's whole body came alive the minute he touched her. His tongue surged in and she wondered if he could taste his own salty essence on her tongue. She'd loved taking his cock in her mouth, adored how much pleasure she could bring to her big strong warrior.

She wished they'd met long ago, wished she'd been the wife by his side when he was hurt. She would have done anything to help him through it. She would have eased the way.

He drew back and pulled his shirt over his head, exposing that chest that always got her hot as hell. Macon was a work of art and a few tiny scars and the loss of most of one leg couldn't change that fact. The imperfections in his body only made him more beautiful to her eyes. She ran her hands over the muscles of his chest, loving the feel of him. His chest was covered in a light dusting of hair. He was so masculine, so tough. His hands were callused and yet they could form the most delicate of confections. That was her Macon in a nutshell. He was a warrior who'd fought and almost died and now he brought joy to others with his art.

"I love you, too, Sir. Macon. My Macon." Being naked with him felt natural. She knew all of their friends were right outside the door. They likely knew exactly what was going on in this room, but Ally didn't care. She wasn't ashamed of what she did with Macon. She'd made plenty of mistakes in her life, but loving this man wasn't one of them and she wouldn't apologize for it. She'd learned a long time ago to take love where she could find. It turned up in unexpected places.

"My Ally," he said with a sure smile. She loved how confident he'd become with her. He slumped down into the big leather chair behind the desk, not bothering to pull up his slacks. His cock was still out and Ally could see it was already stirring back to life. He fished inside his pocket, struggling to pull out something. Condom. "I'm prepared to throw down whenever we can, baby. Come here and sit on my lap."

"I'll get your pants messy." Her female parts were in quite the state. The spanking he'd given her had been enough to get her wet and ready. Sucking him off had done not a thing to solve the problem. She could feel how soft and wet her pussy was.

His eyes narrowed. "I didn't ask you about the state of my clothes. I gave you an order."

And she knew when to comply. She sat right down on his lap, his cock jutting against her hip.

His hands immediately went to her breasts, cupping them with a sigh. "That's better. I think we can definitely move forward with our roles. When we're intimate, I'm going to be in control. You're going to obey me when we're making love."

He leaned forward and pulled her nipple between his lips, giving her the bare edge of his teeth.

The sensation seemed to sizzle through her veins, finding a path between her legs. Macon's pants were definitely going to know she'd been there. It didn't matter. All that mattered was pleasing him in that moment. Everything else could fall to the wayside.

She didn't have to worry about secrets or lies or anything else. She'd found that this was the gift D/s gave her. When Macon took over, she was wholly in the moment and nothing mattered but Macon's needs. By pleasing her Sir, she would please herself. Yes, some people would take advantage of the delicacy of the relationship, but never Macon.

"Yes, Macon." She let her arms drift up around his shoulders, giving him free access to her body. In these moments, her body was his to do with as he wished. Lucky for her, his wishes always included blowing her mind with pleasure.

He switched breasts, licking and tonguing her before sucking it into his mouth and nipping lightly. She shivered, the feeling utterly exquisite. That bite of pain so enhanced her pleasure. She sighed into the sensation, allowing it to flow across her.

"That's what I like to hear. Yes. I want all your yesses, Ally." His hands roamed her body and there was no way to miss the possessiveness that lay behind each and every stroke. "Sanctum is reopening soon. I want you there with me."

Wherever he went, she would be with him. "Of course."

His hand came up to touch her throat. "I want to get you a collar. Nothing crazy, just a necklace that lets other people in the lifestyle know you're mine."

"What about people outside the lifestyle?" She asked the question with a hint of teasing.

"They'll know because of the ring on your finger."

She sat up, her spine straightening. He couldn't have said that. "Macon?"

His hand went to her thigh. He tugged her into the position he wanted her. He hooked her legs over his, spreading them wide. She could feel the metal of his right leg holding her open, contrasting with the left, but she'd decided long ago that she adored every inch of Macon and she loved both his legs, flesh or metal. They were both a part of him.

Her back was to his chest, her body spread out for him.

His hands moved along her body as though he couldn't decide what part to focus on. Everywhere he touched her, warmth spread. "I know it's soon, but I'm going to marry you, Allyson Jones. When you're ready, we'll go to Vegas and make a weekend of it, but you will come back with my ring on your finger. You'll tell me when it's time to go. Make sure, baby, because there won't be any going back. This marriage is forever."

It was all she wanted with him. Forever. It was so selfish. Now was the time to tell him, but she couldn't. She loved him too much to risk it. He never had to know that they'd started out under false pretenses. It was obvious Ronnie had never mentioned that his sister wasn't his biological sibling or that she'd never shared a name with him. She'd always addressed Macon as Sarah Rowe since explaining her relationship would have taken up time and possibly given him a reason to reject speaking with her since she had no real legal standing.

She didn't have to tell him. He would never find out. It was only a little lie that no longer meant anything in the face of how she felt about him. She'd loved Ronnie and her mom, but the pastor had been right. Life was for the living. Ronnie was gone and nothing would bring him back. If the situation hurt Macon too much, he never had to talk about it. She trusted him.

"Can we go on Monday?" They had Mondays off and she was certain if Chef Taggart knew what they were doing he would give them a few days. They could be back for Friday dinner service.

His arms tightened around her. "Are you sure?"

"I love you. I've never loved anyone the way I love you. I've never felt this way. I want to be your wife, your sub, eventually the mother of your babies. I want it all, Macon."

His mouth was right against her ear. "I want it all, too. You should know though that I'm going back to school. There's still a lot I don't know. Sean's agreed to let me take classes a couple of days a week. I want my certification. I want skins on the wall. I'm serious about this profession, but it means a lot of hard work for the next couple of years."

"I'll support you. Whatever we have to do." She would spend her time learning the business end. She'd always liked organizing things. Macon could be the artist and she would make everything else run. Maybe one day they'd have their own bakery. "It's you and me."

They had so little between them. He'd lost everything and she'd never really had anything. So why did she suddenly feel so damn blessed?

"That's how I like it." His hand slid down and it seemed to know exactly where it wanted to go this time. The pad of his finger circled her clit. Over and over and around and around. "Give me one. Come for me and then I'll slide inside you and we'll both come again. And then you'll go out and sit down with our friends and they'll all know I've had you, but that's all right. It's natural and right for me to have you. You belong to me. You're my girl."

"And you belong to me." He was right about that. It was natural. It certainly felt that way. No other man could melt her inhibitions and take her out of her own head the way he could. She was always thinking, always in motion. She'd been that way since she was a child, but things slowed down when she was with Macon. The world stilled and she could relax, giving over to him.

"Yes, I do. I like being your man. Now give me what I want." His finger ran over her clit, pressing with exactly the right amount of strength, and it wasn't long before she was moaning and shoving up against his finger, trying to ride it. She could feel his cock hard against her back and she shivered in anticipation. She would have him inside her soon and she would be complete again. Being with Macon was addictive.

He hit the perfect spot and her body was awash in sweet sensation.

Even as she pulsed with the aftereffects, he was using those big muscled arms of his to move her around.

"Turn around, baby. I want you to ride me." He helped her up and then went to work on the condom. Her knees were weak, but it was a good feeling. She watched as he rolled the condom over his cock.

After they were married she would get on birth control until they were ready for babies. She was going to have them. There was no doubt about that. She wanted a couple of mini-hims running around in the world. Tears struck her eyes as she thought about it. She could have a family again. She could build a life that was good for Macon and their kids. It was everything she'd ever longed for.

"Baby." His hand came out and he seemed to understand what her tears were about. He didn't ask her if she was afraid or offer to stop. He guided her onto his lap, settling her down and sighing as she straddled him and started to lower herself. "I love you so much, Ally."

"I love you, too." She worked her way down. Despite her arousal, he was still so big she had to move slowly to take him. This was what she needed always. This connection was her real home.

She moved up and down, his hands circling her waist and helping to guide her. She held on tight, pressing her chest to his, her nipples rasping against that dusting of hair. His mouth came down on hers, his tongue taking her in a rhythm that matched his cock.

Every movement brought her closer and closer to the edge, but she didn't want it to stop. This was heaven. She surrounded herself with him, lost herself in his arms.

She was getting married. Her and Macon against the world. That was what she'd thought it would be like if she ever found her other half. It would be her and her man against the rough cruel world, but even that had softened when she found Macon. She'd realized the world didn't have to be so bad. She'd found this odd family and she belonged. The world was suddenly filled with possibilities.

"My beautiful girl," he whispered as he picked up the pace. He was lifting her with every thrust. "I bless the day you walked in here."

"Best day of my life." She moved with him and before she was ready, her body was tightening, inner muscles clamping down to milk his cock.

He shuddered and he held on to her as they both went reeling.

She slumped forward, her body exhausted and her mind still for once.

His arms wrapped around her and he held her close. "By this time next week, you're going to be my wife."

She cuddled against him. "I will make sure to send your old one an announcement."

Thirty minutes later she'd ensured that Chef Taggart's office was a model of cleanliness and perfect hygiene. Macon had an extra pair of pants in his gym bag so they were both back to looking somewhat respectable.

She looked at the door Macon had gone out not ten minutes before. Once she opened it, everyone would know.

Except they already knew. They would just know that she knew that they knew.

Screw it. She marched right out. So what if everyone knew she'd made love to the hottest, nicest, most perfect man on the planet.

The minute she walked out the cheering began. She blushed furiously because it seemed like the entire crew was waiting and they'd popped open some champagne.

She looked over at Macon, who walked toward her with a glass in his hand. "You told."

He shrugged. "Deena said she was going to get her shotgun if I didn't make an honest woman out of you."

"I did you a favor," Deena said with a smile. "You shouldn't let a man who makes you scream like that go."

"He makes pies like he makes love," Big Tag said with a shake of his head. "Congratulations to both of you."

Chef Taggart was standing by his big brother. Sean's wife had joined them. Grace was holding their daughter on her hip and she winked their way as her husband stepped up and held up a glass. "To our very first workplace romance to end happily. No, Javi, I'm not counting that socialite you banged in the restroom. She wasn't an employee and the entire relationship only lasted through the first course."

Javier grinned. "But it was a good first course, boss."

Sean shook his head. "You guys are going to kill me. Let's turn this dinner into a celebration. To Macon and Ally."

"To Macon and Ally," the group said in unison.

"Or should we call you Sarah?" a dark voice interrupted.

Adam Miles walked up from the back, his eyes going straight to hers.

Macon's brother knew everything. Her time as Ally was over.

CHAPTER EIGHT

Macon followed his brother into the kitchen, well aware that they were leaving a rather stunned audience in their wake. Ally's hand was firmly in his grasp. He was afraid she would disappear if he didn't keep hold of her.

"Can we go outside? I would love to keep whatever scene is about to play out private," he told his brother, who seemed to have gotten something stuck right up his ass since the last time he'd seen him. Ally had gone pale when Adam had called her Sarah.

Who the hell was Sarah? Was Ally going by her middle name? He wouldn't blame her. He often thought he could have saved himself years of "Macon Bacon" torture if he'd gone by Phillip. Why would Adam be so upset by a name?

Adam nodded briefly and started for the door that led to the back.

Ally tugged on his hand. "I think I should go."

He tugged right back. "You're not going anywhere. Baby, whatever Adam's pissed about, I'll handle it. He can get overprotective at times. Don't worry about it."

"I'm not being overprotective. I'm being exactly the right amount of protective," Adam explained.

Macon led Ally outside and let the door close. He was sure someone would likely try to snoop, but they would be hard pressed to hear them out here. This was a family matter. It looked like his brother had taken his role too seriously and found out about Ally's past. Adam likely had been surprised to find out she had a dad in jail.

"I need to talk to you, Macon." Tears shone in Ally's eyes and she had both hands on his arms, entreating him.

God, when she cried it was like someone kicked him in the gut. "It's going to be fine. Tell me what you need to say." He glared at his big brother. "And you should stay out of it, Adam. I'm grateful, truly grateful for everything you've done, but if you've pulled up dirt on my girlfriend, you've gone too far. She's already told me about her father. I know he's in prison."

Macon should have told Adam. He should have known that Adam would run some kind of check on Ally. But her father's crimes weren't her fault. Not by a long shot. Her childhood had been a chaotic shit storm, but she'd come out of it beautifully.

Adam frowned. "I didn't run a check on Ally. I told you. Sean hired her and that was good enough for me. You did ask me to find out everything I could about Sarah Rowe. Should I tell him or would you like to?"

Adam's last question had been directed at Ally.

Macon's whole body went cold despite the relative warmth of the early evening. He did know a Sarah now that he thought about it. Sarah Rowe had been intent on talking to him. She'd told him in one e-mail that she would get to the bottom of her brother's death no matter what it would cost her.

Would she get in bed with the enemy if it meant finding the truth?

He did the math in his head and quickly realized his Ally was the right age to be Ronnie's sister. She even came from the right part of the world, if she hadn't lied about it.

He slowly let go of her hand and turned to face the woman he loved, wondering if he even knew her name. "Tell me it isn't true."

It was starting to get dark, but he could plainly see her face in the early evening light. The last vestiges of sunlight swept across her hair, illuminating the strands. Her hair normally was a rich brown, but the sunset showed the blonde and red that mixed in. She really was a luscious woman. Was she a liar, too?

Red rimmed her eyes. "I can explain."

There was no explanation. None that he would accept, but he couldn't seem to make himself move. It was a little like after he'd lost his leg. He'd tried to make it move, his brain sending messages to a limb that was no longer there. He stood there trying to process the fact that he'd built a whole world around something that didn't exist, that had never really existed. "Ally" had been a character she'd been playing, a construct built to get close to the target. That's what he was. He wasn't a boyfriend or a fiancé to her. He was the target.

"I'd like to hear an explanation," Adam said, his voice cutting through the dreadfully heavy silence. "Macon asked me to locate Private First Class Rowe's family. I could only come up with his mother, Carla, who died a few months back. When I dug deeper, I discovered a woman named Sarah Allyson Jones had been living with her at the time of her death. Imagine my surprise when I got your records. It might have been better if you'd at least tried. Next time dye your hair or change up your look."

"I wasn't trying to hide," she said. She took a step toward Macon.

He nearly tripped trying to get away from her. He couldn't let her touch him. If she touched him, he would melt like butter. He wouldn't give a damn that she'd lied. He'd tell himself anything so he could keep her. He'd already made a damn fool of himself. What would a gorgeous girl like Allyson want with his pathetic ass?

Sarah. Her name was Sarah.

She stepped back, her face pale. Her eyes wouldn't quite meet his. "You wouldn't answer me. After Ronnie died, my foster mom went a little crazy. She didn't believe the reports on his death. She said Ronnie would never have taken off his helmet or his body armor. He wouldn't have not been wearing it."

No. They were right about that. Ronnie had religiously worn his body armor and his helmet when they were in the field. He'd been wearing it when the Humvee had exploded and the world had gone to shit. It was only after the firefight that they'd been left alone with the sun. Ronnie hadn't been the only one who struggled to survive the intense heat. He could almost feel it now.

He could definitely feel the same hollowness he'd felt that day. He'd looked down and realized he couldn't save himself. He'd been pinned down by the Humvee, his right leg caught. He'd known even if he'd managed to lift the heavy piece off of him, he'd bleed out. The medic had taken one look at him and put his hands up in defeat. The only thing stopping the bleed was the damn metal deep in his thigh.

The whole day was chaos. A few moments after proclaiming Macon would have to wait, the medic—an older man named Johnson—had been shot right through the forehead.

Macon had lain near Johnson's dead body for nearly three days.

He looked at Allyson with new eyes. She'd done a lot for the truth. "I should have answered your calls."

"Macon, it doesn't matter anymore."

He calmed. There would be time for anger later, but right now all he could manage was a cold resignation. She'd likely thought he'd left her no other recourse. "I wasn't sure what to tell you."

"I know you weren't involved," she said quickly. "At the time, we didn't understand the reports and my mom was so sick. She was my foster mom, but I called her Mom. She and Ronnie were my family."

And she was loyal to them. It was a good thing to be. He couldn't compete with her family. "You're wrong, unfortunately. I'm the reason he's dead."

"You are not, Macon," his brother said fiercely.

Macon kind of wished his brother wasn't here to witness this new humiliation, but he deserved it. He'd been a shit to his brother most of his life. He'd chosen the wrong people to believe in. He still did since he'd really believed he had a chance with Ally. Elise had only cared about his father's money. No woman had ever loved him for who he was.

Who was he, anyway? The serious soldier or the pastry chef? The man who'd thrown his brother under the bus because his wife wanted him to or the man who would stand by his brother no matter what?

He wanted to be the man Ally had fallen for. The trouble was Ally didn't exist. The very least he could give her was the truth. She would know what kind of man he was then and she could be satisfied.

"We were out on an assignment. I don't even know everything we were supposed to do. We were going to be told when we got where we were going. We were soldiers. We followed orders. Even as an officer, I was trained to follow the orders of my superiors. They wanted it quiet, I would be quiet. We were meeting someone in a small village outside the desert but to get there we had to go through Taliban territory, hence the quiet. We were a small team. They thought smaller was better. I suspect we were picking up a CIA operative, but I can't be sure."

"Macon, you don't have to," Ally said.

He felt his eyes harden. She was still playing games with him. "Oh, I think I do. I don't want you to have wasted your time."

She shook her head, tears streaming. "Please, Macon."

"Let him get it out, Ally." Adam was quiet, as though he knew how close to the edge Macon was. "He needs to tell this story. You haven't told it to anyone, right?"

"Not even Kai."

"Then don't," Ally said through her tears.

He turned to her. "You came here for this story. You fucked me to get this story. Oh, sweetheart, you're going to get the truth."

"Macon, maybe we should call Kai. We could go to his place and talk about this as a family." Adam seemed awfully reasonable now.

"She's not my family." And she never would be. "I'm going to give her the information she needs and then we can be done."

"I don't want that," Ally said, pleading.

"I don't want to have been lied to for weeks. I guess we can't always get what we want. You want to know what happened to your brother? Shit happened. It happened to all of us. We were deep in the desert when we realized we had a low tire. Rowe and I got out and patched it. The driver liked to play pranks. Asshole kid. He pulled away when we tried to get back in. It was a joke. I believe I threatened to kill the little fucker if he did it again. Which he did. That was when he hit an IED. Blew the fuck out of us. I got caught under a heavy piece of the vehicle. I was pinned down. A couple of us were. That's when they showed up. Taliban. They started to pick us off. The stupid piece that took my leg provided cover for me. Same for Rowe. He was pinned down next to me, but it was both his legs. At some point they decided to come and do some up-close fighting. There were only three of them. Two of them were kids. I killed a kid. Couldn't have been more than fourteen. I shot him in the back before he could take out Kellison. Didn't matter. The other kid got him. Rowe and I took out the other two despite the fact that we couldn't walk, couldn't move. We could still shoot."

"Macon," Ally began.

Adam held up a hand. "Don't. He needs to do this."

He ignored them both. He wanted to get it all over with. He wanted to walk away. His first instinct was to leave, but he was going to fight that. His brother hadn't done anything wrong. He could at least still have his brother in his life. But no Ally.

126

"It got quiet after that. Really quiet. Rowe and I were the only ones left alive. We did what we were trained to do. We took stock of what we had. Neither one of us could move. I managed to get a tourniquet around my leg, but I couldn't move the Humvee. We had a couple of energy bars and one bottle of water between us. We rationed it, but there wasn't much left after a day and a half. We knew there was more. I could even see a bottle of it, but I couldn't get to it. At one point I tried to use my knife. I tried to saw my own damn leg off so I could get to it, but I kept passing out."

Ally was weeping freely now, but he was strangely numb. He didn't even want to hold her. It was all bullshit. She was crying for her brother. He thought about all the times he'd left her alone in his house. Had she searched his computer, his phone, his paperwork? She wouldn't have found anything. She hadn't found anything or she likely would have hit the road by now.

"On the second day we realized we had no idea if anyone at all was coming. Our mission had been secretive." His stomach rolled as he thought about some of the things he wasn't saying. He didn't mention that the vultures had shown up. They'd been smaller than American vultures, but no less hungry. He'd tried to get them off his teammates, but he'd been useless. He'd sat back and waited to die. "If the Agency was involved, we could have been written off. We had no idea. We were dumb and utterly at the mercy of the elements. Helpless. I'd never thought of myself that way before. I was completely helpless and I started to believe that dehydration would get us before anyone would think to look for us. If they looked for us."

He'd wondered if anyone would even care that he was gone. Elise would take his insurance and buy a better husband. He didn't have kids. He'd cut off ties with the one brother who might have given a shit.

"He talked about you." If he was going to tell the truth, he was going to tell all of it. "He loved you. He said you saved him when he was a dumb kid getting the shit kicked out of him in high school. He never once mentioned you weren't his blood. You were his sister and he loved you."

"I loved him, too."

That was obvious. "We knew the water wouldn't keep us alive for long. I like to think that he thought he was in worse shape, that he thought he was doing the right thing."

Her hand covered her mouth as she choked down a sob. She'd obviously figured out the secret he'd kept, but he had to say it.

"During the second night, Private First Class Rowe put his service pistol to his head and he pulled the trigger." He could still hear that sound. He'd come to, his own gun in hand, thinking it was all over. Another group of Taliban had found them. He'd been surprised at how little it scared him. He was ready to fight because it was what he did, but he wasn't sure he really cared. There was nothing in his life worth fighting for.

And then he'd realized what had happened.

"I ran out of water the next day. The chopper came for me that night. I don't know if we could have survived or not, but I think he made a triage choice. I think he decided I had a better shot without him."

"Or the pain got to be too much for him," Adam said.

Macon shook his head. "We were numb by then. At least I was. He'd said something about making the right choices at the right times. We were talking about religion. It's funny what you talk about when you're two men dying in a desert. That was what religion meant to him. The right choices. I sometimes think I should have done it. I should have pulled that trigger and given him the shot at living. He had more to live for."

He was numb now, as oddly unfeeling as he'd been back then. Somehow Ally's tears couldn't seem to reach him. It was like discovering her lies had pulled the soft part of him out and left him gutted, hollow and only animated by the survival instinct.

Had he recently stood in the middle of Top and toasted his engagement to Ronnie's sister? How long would she have played it out? She certainly couldn't have meant to go through with the wedding. Did she want revenge? If she did, she'd gotten a good one because he was broken and wasn't sure he would be fixed again. He'd thought Elise's betrayal had hurt? It was nothing like this. He couldn't even muster real anger.

"Why didn't you tell the Army?" Ally's back was against the wall as though she needed it or she'd fall. "None of that was in the report. That was why Mom was so upset. She knew something was off with that report. She went a little crazy after Ronnie died. She was sick and so lost. She grabbed on to that report. If she'd known…"

"She wouldn't have received death benefits," Adam finished for her.

"Private First Class Rowe received the regular hundred thousand for dying in the line of duty, but he'd maxed out his SGLI."

"We all do," Macon said. This conversation was coming to a close and it couldn't be soon enough for him. "It doesn't pay in the case of suicide—not for as short a time as he'd been in. I often wonder if he knew that. He'd only had that policy for eighteen months. He sacrificed himself, but they would have seen it as suicide. When the extraction unit came for me, they covered it up. They knew why he'd done it. It was easy to see. No one wanted his family to suffer. You deserved the money and we weren't going to allow some paper pusher to make that decision. Not that it helped. How did you end up living in your car? You should have had half a million."

She covered her mouth again and sobbed. The sound made his spine straighten. He wasn't going to hold her. No matter how much his instinct told him to. His instincts sucked or he would have figured out her game before now.

Adam had softened. He moved to her side and Macon was a little grateful that someone could be there for her. "Your mother was in an assisted living facility, wasn't she?"

She nodded. "Medicare wouldn't pay because she suddenly had too much money. I didn't know what else to do. She needed the care."

Macon laughed, the sound bitter as hell even to his own ears. "The facility ate through it until Medicare took over. What a fucking joke. He died for his country and his mother got eaten alive by it. Nice. Well, that explains why you're broke."

He couldn't kick her out. Not if the money was really gone. He owed it to Ronnie. They hadn't been the best of friends, but they'd worked together and they'd shared something very few people ever did.

It struck him again that Ronnie had been the one who should have survived. The half a million would have thrilled Elise, and his father would have been infinitely prouder of him if he'd died in combat. Another Miles hero to put on the family wall. If he'd been the one to die, Allyson wouldn't be weeping like she was never going to stop.

"Adam, could I have a moment alone with her?"

His brother frowned. "I don't think that's such a great idea. Macon, I got mad. I thought she was sending that PI after you to hurt you, but I think I misjudged her. I didn't handle this well. I really think we should all go home and cool off and talk about this."

Ally shook her head. "The first week I had a little money, I rehired the PI who had worked for my mom. He was supposed to ask a few questions. I haven't paid him anything since. I didn't intend to ever again."

"I need a moment alone with Allyson," he said in his firmest voice.

"Don't do anything you're going to regret," his brother said as he stepped back into the restaurant.

And left him alone with the only woman he'd ever really loved. Hell, he hadn't even understood what the word meant until she'd showed up. Too bad it had been one sided. "I think you should stay in the guesthouse until you have enough money for a decent apartment."

The desolation in her eyes damn near killed him. "But you won't be there, will you?"

"No. My brother has a guest room. I'll stay there. I'll head home with him and be out of your way in an hour or so." They wouldn't have to see much of each other. Even at work. She was in the front of the house and he was in the back. He could come in early and get most of what he needed to done. He could leave at close or right before.

Or he could go home. He could accept his place. He wouldn't accept Elise. Nothing could make him do that, but he could go home. Once his father understood no reporter was coming for him to trash the family name, he would likely take him back and the money would open up again. He could shuffle his way numbly through life. He would have to work for his father, of course. It wouldn't matter.

"Macon, please listen to me," she said.

He held out a hand. "I'm not angry. I understand why you did it. I should have spoken to you. It was hard to do it, but I owed it to you and your mother. I failed. I wish you well, Allyson."

He started to go.

"Please talk to me. Please don't leave me," she pleaded.

If he stayed he would beg her and he didn't have anything but his pride left. Without another look back, he slipped through the door.

He'd done his duty. He'd given her what she'd come for and now it was time to move on.

And forget her.

* * * *

Allyson walked into the restaurant well aware that she looked like hell. Her face was red and puffy. She didn't cry pretty. There wasn't anything she could do about it. She'd sat out there for thirty minutes after Macon had walked away from her. She'd cried and Deena had come out to hug her. She'd asked what had happened, but Ally had simply cried. After a while, she'd asked Deena if she could be alone. She'd been able to see how reluctant her friend was, but she'd done it.

She was going to miss Deena and Serena and all the friends she'd made at Top. She'd made more genuine friends here in the few months she'd been in Dallas than in the years before. It had been a good place to be.

She wondered if they all hated her now.

It would be easier to slink away, but she was done with easy. She owed Chef Taggart an explanation. He'd given her a job when he shouldn't have. She would give him the courtesy of quitting to his face. Of course, he might make it easy on her. He might fire her the minute she walked back in the door.

The dinner was going on as planned, though she thought the dining room was a lot quieter than it usually was. She could smell ribs and roasted potatoes, but she couldn't eat a thing. Macon's Napoleons looked perfect. Not that she would be invited to join, but she would miss it.

The room went silent as she walked in. It occurred to her that she was interrupting a family dinner. That's what these people had become. Chef Taggart sat at one end and his brother at the other. They were partners in Top. Big Tag was the silent partner who often said he'd only put money into the business for the free pies, but it was easy to see that the Taggart brothers depended on each other.

Her brother was dead and the only man she'd ever loved hated her now. She was back on the street again. Story of her life.

Every eye was looking her way. She noticed Serena and Jake weren't among them. The Miles family had closed ranks.

"Ally." Deena stood up. Tiffany and Jenni stood up with her. All of her server coworkers, it seemed, were ready to talk to her at least.

Ally shook her head and Deena nodded. They all sat back down.

Ian Taggart's eyes narrowed as he looked at her. His wife had joined him, but it looked like the twins had been put down for a nap. "You broke the pie maker."

Charlotte Taggart slapped at her husband's muscular arm. "Ian.

Tact, please."

"Baby, I don't have any of that," he admitted. "She broke the dude who makes the pies. She's gotta fix him."

She didn't even want to get into an argument with Ian Taggart. He kind of scared her. She didn't think he would be impressed with her little hammer. She turned to the man she'd come to talk to. "Chef Taggart, I'm so sorry to interrupt. Could I please have a word with you?"

He stood up, dropping his napkin, but his wife reached for his hand. He leaned over and she whispered something in his ear. Grace Taggart handed over their toddler girl. She'd been sitting in her mother's lap, but she seemed content to go with her father.

"I'll handle this," Grace said. She stood up, smoothing out her skirt and nodding Ally's way. "Let's talk in the office."

She was surprised but followed behind the gorgeous redhead. Did she not want Ally alone with her husband? What exactly had Macon said when he left? She shouldn't be surprised that he'd talked bad about her, but she was. Somehow, even though she knew she'd hurt him, she hadn't expected him to lash out. She'd come to know such gentleness from the big bear of a man, but she supposed that was only for the women who were worthy.

Grace closed the door behind her and the world got eerily quiet.

It was best to get it over with so she could get her things and leave. She wasn't going to take him up on his offer to stay in the guesthouse. No way. She would pick a road and drive all night, and sometime tomorrow she would be somewhere else. Hell, maybe she'd be someone else. "Mrs. Taggart, I'm afraid I need this to be my last day. I'm sorry I can't give you two weeks' notice."

"Unacceptable." Grace sat down in her husband's chair. The very one she'd so recently made love to Macon in. "You did a good job cleaning this place. It smells like citrus. You'll have to tell me what you use. I can never get the sex smell out of Ian's office. Sean thinks it's funny to play on Ian's desk when Ian's out of town. I've told Charlotte I'll give her the keys to the castle, but the twins don't like to sleep much so she hasn't had a chance for revenge yet."

Grace gestured to one of the two seats in front of the desk, but Ally stayed on her feet. "I'm sorry about using the office. We really did clean it and well, it certainly won't ever happen again."

"It won't with that attitude." Grace frowned. "Please have a seat,

Allyson. Or do you prefer Sarah? I was sorry to hear about your mother and your brother. This must be a very difficult time for you."

She thought she'd gotten over the shock of having people know her secret. "Macon told you everything."

"No, Macon didn't say a word. He walked out without speaking to anyone. I've known that your name was Sarah Allyson Jones of Ashwick, Georgia, since Ian did a background check on you a few weeks into your employment. We made the connection between you and Macon a long time ago."

Now she took the seat, her knees too weak to stand. "Why didn't you tell him?"

Grace considered her for a moment. "I argued that we should. Sean and Ian wanted to watch you. They wanted to see what you would do. That's why they didn't tell Adam. He would have blown your cover. He did, in the end, of course. Sean thought that if we'd told Macon in the beginning, he simply would have left. It's not hard to figure out that man was hiding some kind of secret. I thought you were investigating him."

"I was," she admitted.

"You did a horrible job, hon." Grace pointed to the bookshelf. It was filled with cookbooks. "There's a nice security camera hidden up there. Don't worry, it's only turned on after hours. It's aimed at the safe where he keeps the cash. It was definitely turned off this afternoon. Sean did have it on one night a few months back. He wanted to know why you were really here."

She searched her memory. "I don't remember anything that would have been interesting on camera."

"That's my point. Sean's trap didn't work on you," Grace explained. "It was turned on a night when Sean asked you to stay late. He then took a very long phone call out in the alley. He left his door wide open and the personal files of every employee were sitting right on his desk. He had to ask you to grab him a notepad off his desk to get you to go inside."

Now she remembered. "He said he was arguing with a vendor. He was outside for a long time. I saw the files."

"And you looked down at them and pulled Macon's file. And then you replaced it and walked away without ever glancing inside. Why?"

"Because it didn't matter by then. I knew what I needed to know about him. I knew he was a good man." Those damn tears were back and she wondered how long it would be before she stopped crying over him. "I came here because I wanted to ask him about my brother's death, but then I got to know him and I couldn't."

Grace stood up and moved around the desk, sitting in the chair beside her. "Why didn't you tell him?"

"I was scared. I didn't want to lose him." But she had and she already felt the loss like a hole had opened in her lungs and she couldn't breathe anymore.

"You had to know someone would find out."

"Why? There weren't any legal ties to my mom or brother. Why couldn't I call myself Ally and start over?" It had been a good plan that had gone so very wrong.

"How many times have you started over?"

She shrugged. "A couple."

"I think you've made a habit out of running away," Grace said softly. "But sometimes you have to stand your ground to start over. Sometimes running away isn't the answer. Do you love him?"

Ally nodded, unable to speak.

"Then leaving is the worst thing you can do."

"It's my fault."

A look of determination set in Grace's hazel eyes. "Then be woman enough to stand up and admit it. Take responsibility and then atone. You don't have to leave, but you need to figure something out. You need to decide if you're good for him. You can't be good for him if you're hundreds of miles away. I've seen that man come alive since he started dating you. He was happy and he can be happy again. He needs time and patience from you. But the last thing he needs is distance and your self-doubt. Do you believe in your heart that you're good for him?"

She believed that she loved him. She knew she'd do anything it took to help him achieve his dreams. She was his natural partner, a lover who fit his needs. She'd spent a lifetime thinking she wasn't good enough. It would be simple to fall into that familiar pattern again, but it wasn't what Macon needed. She'd seen the way his shoulders had slumped, how his hand had unconsciously gone to his damaged leg as if he could hide it. He didn't think she'd ever loved him. When he'd thought she loved him, he'd stood taller, walked with more pride. She'd given that to him.

She had to find a way to give it to him again. "I am good for him."

"If you love him, you fight for him."

There was only one problem. "I don't think he wants me anymore."

Grace sighed and for a moment it looked like she was lost in some memory. "He doesn't know what he wants right now, honey. He's hurt and angry and willing to burn everything down because of it. I should know. I've been there. Do you know why I married Sean?"

"Because you love him."

"Yes, obviously. But Sean hurt me in the beginning. I'm with him today because he was patient and he apologized and he never stopped telling me he loved me. He kept saying it until I believed it. I think Macon needs to hear that. He needs to know that you won't leave. Even when it gets ugly. He needs to know that your love isn't a currency. You're not trying to buy something from him."

That was all Macon had known. "His wife wanted money and a place in their society."

"And what do you want?"

She searched her heart. There was an easy answer, but it wasn't the truest one. She wanted Macon, but there was something she wanted even more. When she really went deep she discovered what she wanted beyond everything else. "I want Macon to be happy. I want him to have a good life."

Grace put her hand over Ally's. "Oh, honey. That means you're really in love and that is worth fighting for. You made a mistake. A big one. That's not going to go away easy, but it's time to stop running. It's time to stand. It's time to say this is my home and I won't leave."

"And if he still hates me?"

"Then at least you found a home." Grace stood. "Now let's go and eat and we'll talk this out. That's what families do."

She was crying again, but it was all right. It was better than all right. It was time to fight.

Late in the night she locked the door behind her. She looked around the guesthouse and knew she was alone. There was no Macon in the kitchen puttering around with some new experiment. He wasn't in the shower or out jogging. He was gone and she knew it before she checked his closet.

She moved through the house, reliving every moment with him. How could she prove that she loved him? How could she make him believe?

When she got to the kitchen she nearly broke down again. This was where he'd first really kissed her, where they'd decided to move forward. Where she'd lied to him. Where she'd learned to love him.

She noticed a book sitting by the stove. Macon's mother's recipe book. He'd left it. She would have to make sure it got back to him because she knew how precious it was, but first she opened it. Maybe it would give her some kind of look into the woman who had given birth to the man she loved. Macon had only told her that his real mother had died young and he'd been left with a cold father and a stepmother who hadn't wanted children.

She flipped through the pages. The recipes weren't elaborate. This was the cookbook of a housewife, a simple memory book of easy meals and treats likely passed on from her mother and her grandmother. They were written in a neat feminine hand and her eyes teared as she noticed each recipe had one ingredient in common. The last ingredient listed for each dish was the same. Love.

Somehow, in that moment, she could practically feel this woman reach through time and offer her kindness, asking her to be patient with her boy, to give him what he truly needed. Love. Somehow, someway this book was meant for her. She was the next in line. Macon might be an artist, but she would be the one to cook for their children.

She wiped her eyes and selected a recipe. Snickerdoodles. They would be a good start. She found the ingredients and got to work.

CHAPTER NINE

M_T

Macon stared at the pie on the counter. It was the sixth offering this week. It sat there with its slightly crooked lattice crust. She was impatient with it. That type of crust required a very precise hand. The presentation was less than perfect and he couldn't help but want a taste.

But then he also wanted a taste of the woman who had made it.

Why the hell wouldn't she leave him alone?

"Oh, what do we have today?" Jake was straightening his tie as he entered the kitchen. His eyes had immediately gone to the counter.

"Apple," Serena said as she offered Jake a mug of coffee. "It was still warm when Macon brought it in so I think she's having trouble sleeping."

Was she sitting up all night baking?

Jake took the mug from her and his free hand wound around her waist, pulling her close. "I don't know about that. All I know is while Ally makes a mean pie, it's not yours, baby. You've got the best pie in the entire world and I can never get enough of it."

He took his wife's mouth in a hungry kiss.

And Macon rolled his eyes because Serena didn't bake. The last week had been a horrible trial. Living with his brother, Jake, and Serena meant continually watching either Jake or Adam trying to get into their wife's pants. They were like horny teenage boys. And Tristan pooped a lot. The kid was cute, but damn he could stink up a room, and half the time Macon was left holding a grinning baby with a diaper full of poo because the three of them were getting it on now that they had a babysitter. They'd treated him like glass that first night, but after two days of tiptoeing around him, his family seemed to figure out that double penetration was way easier when someone was watching the baby and Uncle Macon was put to work.

He'd spent most of his time sitting with Tristan and talking about Ally. That kid knew more about his relationship with Ally than anyone should. Luckily, he just drooled a lot and tried to eat his own fist.

This was what he was reduced to. His only confidant was a baby and the woman of his dreams was a yard away making dessert after dessert and leaving it on his doorstep. He'd woken up the morning after he'd discovered her lie and there had been a plate of cookies waiting for him. She'd wrapped it in foil with a note. *For Macon.*

Nothing else. He hadn't touched them. He'd brought them in and put them on the counter and walked away. When he'd gotten to work and found her there, he'd ignored her completely. He'd kept his head down and done his job and she'd done hers. She hadn't sought him out, hadn't come by his station. The one time they'd locked eyes accidently, she'd given him the saddest smile like she'd known he wasn't playing her games anymore.

He'd gotten a ride with Eric and thought it was all over.

He'd been greeted the next day with a vanilla cake with simple chocolate frosting. *For Macon.*

How much did she think he ate?

"Hey, you two. How about I get in on that action?" Adam was carrying Tristan as he entered the kitchen. He looked down at the counter. "Nice. I'll take that up to the office. Ian is starting to think this argument between you and Ally is the best thing to happen to him."

McKay-Taggart was benefitting from the end of what had to be the shortest engagement in history. Adam or Jake simply picked up whatever he left on the counter and took it to work and put the pie or cake or cookies in the break room where it was devoured by hungry agents.

Jake stepped back and took Tristan from Adam, hauling the baby up and giving him kisses that had him giggling at his dad. "Ian wants to put in a request for more lemon."

"Ian can bite me," Macon said, his surliness showing. He wasn't going to march across the lawn and encourage Ally.

"I would watch out," Serena replied. "Ian likes to bite. I'll go out and ask Ally if she can put something lemony in her rotation."

This whole conversation irritated him. "When did Ally become your damn personal baker? Excuse me. Sarah. Let's use her real name."

"She prefers Ally. It's her middle name," Serena explained. "She really wants to make a break from her past."

He narrowed his eyes, staring at his sister-in-law. "And how would you know that?"

If Serena was intimidated, he couldn't tell. "I went over to see if she was all right. You know, only a couple of times. A day." She shook her head and planted her foot on the hardwood floor, pointing a judgmental finger his way. "She's my friend. Just because she made one phenomenally stupid mistake doesn't change that. If I cut people out of my life because they did stupid things, I would have no friends. And yes, I'm looking at you, Jacob Dean."

Now Jake was staring at Macon with what Macon liked to think of as his satanic, soul-claiming face. He was fairly certain Jake used that face right before he killed people. "Thanks for reminding her, brother. My day's blown. Let's get to the office, buddy."

Three days a week, Tristan went to the office with his dads when they weren't out on assignment. Ian Taggart had turned one of the unused conference rooms into a daycare center. The other two days Tristan stayed home with Mom. They liked to say it was the best of both worlds. Serena got to work and be with her boy and so did Jake and Adam.

He wasn't going to have a kid like Tristan. And it was all Ally's fault. Before Adam could pick up the pie, Macon grabbed it. It was time to show Ally that he wasn't playing around.

"Tell Ian the bakery's closed."

"I think he's moved into his anger phase," Jake whispered to Adam.

"Kai warned us this would happen." Adam was frowning his way.

He clutched the stupid, probably-had-too-much-cinnamon-in-it pie. Had she even used ice water for the crust or had she thought cold tap would be enough? "You're the one who started this, brother. You want to tell me why you're looking at me like I'm the bad guy? And why is Kai saying anything? Does he not understand patient-client confidentiality?"

He was really tired of everyone having an opinion. He'd heard it from Eric and Javier and the line chefs. *Poor Ally. She looks tired. She seems so sad.*

The other servers had stopped talking to him with the exception of Deena, who still communicated but seemed to think four-letter words and dirty hand gestures were appropriate.

He was the fucking victim here.

"I called Kai because I was worried about you," Adam explained. "You've completely shut down. And don't think I am not fully aware of the part I played. I acted hastily. I was trying to protect you but I should have brought the problem to the group and figured out how to handle it. Macon, sometimes it's more important why a person lied than that they lied in the first place. I think we should talk about this."

"I don't want to talk. I want to do my job and live my life and I want to do it without that woman." He couldn't even say her name sometimes.

But he could dream about her. He dreamed about her every single night. He saw her gorgeous face as she worked over him, her lips mouthing the words "I love you."

"I'm going to get Tristan in his car seat," Jake said, his face grim. "Please come help me, baby."

Serena nodded and followed him out, leaving him alone with his brother.

"You're not only mad at her," Adam began. "You're mad at me and I don't blame you."

"I'm not mad at you." Adam had done what any good brother would have done. He'd brought him the truth. He'd shown him the facts and saved him from making a damn fool of himself.

"Of course you are and until you acknowledge it, it's going to be difficult around here."

Well, he should have seen that coming. "I'll find a place of my own then. I wouldn't want to make your life difficult."

"You see. Right there. You take everything I say in the worst possible manner. I don't want you to leave. I want you to talk to me."

"There's nothing to talk about. I'm not angry. Hell, I'm not really even angry with her. She did what she needed to do to get the information she wanted. I suppose now she thinks she's found a cushy place to land and she doesn't want to lose it."

"Are you talking about living in our guesthouse?"

"It's nice, especially to a woman like her. She's never had much of anything so she's hungry for some comfort and she'll fuck the first guy who can give it to her." It was the only explanation as to why she was still trying.

Adam's eyes rolled. "Yeah, buddy. You're a catch. You live in your brother's guesthouse, have zero money saved, and don't even own a car. She's totally after your wealth."

But Ally had a car. Between them they had a place to stay, a heap of junk car, and three and a quarter legs. Ally wouldn't let him forget that quarter leg. It was an asset, she would say. Had she said it to get close to him?

"Fuck you, Adam." He wasn't going down that road again.

Adam nodded. "Yes, that's better. Yell at me. Get it out. I know we were taught to shove everything down, but that's not what we should do. You don't cure a boil by pushing it under the skin. You lance that fucker and let it all hang out. That's the only way you're going to heal. Say it. Tell me how I screwed up your life."

He shook his head stubbornly. "You didn't. You helped me. Although I will admit you're annoying me now. If you want me to leave, I wish you would say it."

"Where would you go?"

"Home. I talked to Dad last night. He's willing to offer me a job."

Adam's jaw dropped. "You've got to be kidding me. You're willing to go back there? To a father who dumped you at your lowest moment?" His brother's expression was so hurt, Macon almost took the words back. "And you say you're not angry with me."

Adam shook his head and walked out toward the garage.

He didn't understand. Adam had always been the smart one. He'd been the rebel, able to shove aside everything. Macon had given in. He'd chosen comfort over Adam when they were younger. He'd let Ronnie blow his own head off. He'd been stupid enough to believe Ally's lies.

At least he could do one thing. He could break his silence with Ally. She hadn't taken the hint. He clutched the pie and strode to the backdoor. All he could think about as he made it to the grass was telling Ally he didn't need her damn pie. He could make his own pie. Hell, he could buy a pie if he really wanted one, but he wasn't ever touching her pie again. He wasn't going to taste her sweetness and eat a piece like a starving man. No. She'd ruined pie for him, or maybe it had been the numerous sexual references his brother seemed to make about pie, but it didn't matter. Pie sucked. He didn't eat pie any more so she could keep her fucking sweet ass pie to herself. Or give it away to the next idiot. He didn't care.

He tripped, not looking where he was going, and cursed his fucking leg as he fell to the ground. His not leg. His fucked up, blown to shit body that only one woman had ever really wanted.

The pie fell to the ground, glass pan cracking and sending the insides all over the grass.

He tried to get up, but he stumbled again, his leg unable to move the way he needed it to.

"Macon!" Ally's face suddenly loomed over him.

And he wanted to hurt her the way she'd hurt him.

* * * *

Ally had seen him walking across the yard like a man on a mission. She'd taken a deep breath because she'd been waiting for it. She'd been waiting for the moment when he finally confronted her. She'd thought it would go one of two ways. He'd either realize he forgave her and couldn't stay away a moment longer or he would realize he couldn't stand two more seconds without telling her what a lying bitch she was.

From the look in his eyes, she'd been willing to bet he'd chosen door number two.

But it hadn't mattered what his intentions were once she'd seen him fall.

She threw open the door and raced across the space between them. She hadn't cared that she was wearing nothing but a tank top and a pair of boxer shorts. She ran to get to him. "Macon!"

She dropped to her knees.

He was on his back, his eyes closed. His handsome face was set in mulish lines. "Go away."

"Let me help you." She reached for his hand and the minute she did, his closed around it.

His eyes came open and she could see the blazing emotion in them. He was so mad, so angry. God, she was afraid of him in that moment. "You won't go away then you get what you deserve."

He tugged her down on top of him and then rolled his big body over, pinning her down. She caught a glimpse of his face before he took her mouth. There was no kindness in this kiss, but it didn't matter. It was still Macon and the minute his lips met hers, it started a wildfire low in her gut. Her whole body softened.

His tongue plundered, his hands gripping her wrists over her head. She was completely immobilized, held down as he savaged her mouth.

She managed to get her legs spread, wanting nothing more than to feel his erection against her core. He was dressed in sweats and a T-shirt, likely getting ready for either PT or a workout. The thin layers of clothing that separated them did nothing to obscure the feel of his lengthening cock. He grew by the second and she responded.

She wrapped her arms around him. If he needed this, needed to be rough with her, she could handle it. She could take everything he had to give. She'd spent day after day praying he would get that hard glint in his eyes and order her someplace private where he could spank her for lying to him. If he would do that, be the Dom he'd told her he wanted to be, then she would know there was hope.

Taking out his anger through sex was certainly a better way than taking it out by yelling at her. She didn't care. All she knew was they had to break through his rage.

He ground his cock against her, the big erection hitting her clit. It didn't take much to make her ready for him. In the time they'd lived together, he'd trained her to expect pleasure from him, and her body was ready. Night after night she'd gone to their lonely bed and lain awake thinking about all the ways they'd made love. And it was love. He might be telling himself it was all about sex, but it wasn't. It wasn't even about sex now. Even as he thrust his hand under her shirt and started to cup her breasts, she knew emotion was riding him. This wasn't lust. It was dominance and possession. She'd stripped him of his newfound confidence and she had to find a way to get it back.

"I love you."

His head came up. "Don't you fucking say that to me again."

"I can keep my mouth shut, but it doesn't change the truth." She wasn't going to back down. This was too important.

"Do you love me enough to let me fuck you again?" He said the word "love" with a nasty twist of his mouth, like it was something distasteful.

"Yes."

His hips moved, sliding his cock along her core. If they'd been naked, he would have been inside her. "What does that make you, Sarah?"

She was sure he would use all kinds of nasty words on her. They wouldn't mean anything. He was a wounded animal and they tended to bite the hands of the people who healed them because they didn't know any better. She'd had two long talks with Adam since the day Macon had left her. He'd shown up on her doorstep—his doorstep really—the morning after the debacle and demanded to know why she was still here. He'd offered her cash to leave and when she wouldn't, he'd finally sat down and listened to her. And then he'd spoken. He'd told her about his and Macon's childhood. There had been no softness, no love. Macon didn't know how to react. He was just learning and she'd made him stumble in a brutal fashion.

She reached up and brushed back his dark hair. "What does that make me? A woman in love with a man."

He growled and rolled off her. His back was on the grass, one arm thrown over his eyes. "Go away, Ally."

She sat up, staring down at him. "I can't."

"Why the fuck not?"

"Because I think this is my home." Because she loved the people around her. She loved what she'd found here. "Macon, I'm so sorry for not telling you who I am, but I think I fell in love with you the minute I saw you. I was afraid I would lose you."

"You never had me."

"Of course I did. I think we were more real together than we've ever been apart. I like who I was when I was with you."

His eyes opened slightly. "A liar?"

She sighed. "A woman. I've been a scared little girl for so long, but when I was with you, I was finally a woman. The last of that scared girl is gone now so you should know that while I think I'll love you forever, if you can't find it in your heart to forgive me, I'll move on eventually."

She'd thought about it for the whole two weeks they'd been separated. Every day that had gone by felt like they were further and further apart. She'd even heard he was talking to his father again. He'd told one of the line chefs he might be going back home to New York. She'd come to a decision. Her life couldn't be over because one man refused to forgive her. She had to value herself. She had to be meaningful and that meant forgiving. Forgiving him for being too broken. Forgiving herself for screwing up.

"Move on now. I want you out. I'll give you the money for a down payment. I want you gone," he said stubbornly.

"I don't want to leave."

"It's my family. I get to stay. I want you gone by this weekend and find another job."

Now he was pushing her too far. "I understand that you're angry, Macon. I really do. I understand that you're backed into a corner and you don't know how to do anything but fight your way out. I'm willing to take some abuse. I really am. I did this. I'm the at-fault party, but if you think for a second I'll let you force me out of a place that's good for me, you're wrong. Maybe you could have before now. Maybe before I met you, loved you, you could have bullied me right out of town, but I'm a different person than the street rat who showed up on your doorstep. I never once used you for information. I gave that up about two weeks in. I slept with you because I loved you. I slept with you because I've never wanted a man the way I want you."

"I can't look at you and not see your brother. Do you understand that? You're alone because he chose me over himself. Think about it for two seconds, Sarah, and you'll be as mad at me as I am at you."

She sighed. He understood nothing. "My name is Allyson and he did what his heart told him to do. And Macon, he didn't leave me alone. He left me with you. I don't believe in coincidence. I believe we walk a road no matter how twisted and broken it is. It leads us where we need to be. We're the ones who choose to stop, who stay in a place too long or simply give up moving down the road. Ronnie died and I loved him and his death led me to a man I love even more. So get up and walk with me. If you don't, I'm going to start again. I'll go without you if I have to because I believe in you, but I recently realized that I believe in me, too. I won't quit. I love my job and I can go to school during the day."

Besides attempting to make all the recipes in his mother's cookbook, she'd spent her time trying to figure out her next move. Her whole life had been about running from the past or taking care of someone else. It was time to build a future with or without Macon.

"School? College?"

"Not all of us made it through West Point. Yeah. I think I'm going to school. I'm going to study business. At first I wanted to because I thought I could help you. You'll want your own bakery one day. I thought I could learn how to run it so you could concentrate on what you love. Well, maybe I can do it for someone else. I'm learning the restaurant industry. Maybe I can manage one someday. I don't have to be a street rat the rest of my life. I can be more."

His face softened and for a moment she thought he would say something sweet to her. Then he closed his eyes again. "I don't care what you do. If you don't leave, then I will."

Tears threatened again. "All right then."

He huffed and the steel was back in his eyes when he looked at her. "So what? You standing around waiting to help the cripple up?"

She was thinking about kicking him in the ribs. "Nope. I'm sure you'll manage fine all on your own. Good-bye, Macon. I'll be out of the house tonight."

"Tell me how much the down payment is."

If he was going to be an ass, she definitely wasn't taking a dime from him. She was sure it would reassure him she was some kind of gold digger. "Nothing. I'll manage."

"I don't want you sleeping in that car again, Allyson," he called out.

"I guess what you want doesn't matter anymore." She walked away, her soul sagging. She watched him through the window. Eventually he managed to struggle to his feet and go back inside.

He didn't need her help and she was beginning to believe she didn't need him.

* * * *

Macon strode into Chef Taggart's office with his gut in a knot. It was Friday night after dinner service. He had to catch his boss before he disappeared to go to whoever's house was hosting Sanctum this week. Friday nights were a standing playdate between Sean and Grace Taggart.

He needed to get this shit over with. He couldn't take too much more of watching Ally with her sad eyes and luscious body.

Not that she'd been too sad earlier in the afternoon. She'd stood over him and told him off. Like she had a right to do that. Like two weeks was too much time to ask for. Not that he'd asked for time. He didn't care. He didn't care that she'd been so beautiful telling him she believed in herself, that she'd made plans to stand behind him, to be his partner, but if he was an idiot, she'd move on.

Nope. He didn't care. He wanted her to move on. He was going to do the same. What she'd done was unforgivable. In his family, you didn't get a second chance. You got it right or you were done.

Was he really hearing his father's voice in his head? Was that what he wanted his life to come to?

"You wanted to see me?" Sean Taggart sat behind his desk, going over the nightly reports. "Make it quick. We're due at Ian's in an hour."

"I'll pass tonight."

"Oh, okay. I guess you heard Ally's there. You know just because you're not together doesn't mean you should stop going to the club."

He stopped, his heart clenching. "What do you mean Ally's going?"

Sean sat back. "She's asked Ian if she can be accepted as a trainee. Smart girl. She showed up at Ian's office with a lemon icebox pie about a week ago and negotiated so she doesn't have to pay fees. She's taking care of the kids for three months twice a week and then training on Saturday nights. Tomorrow is her first training night. I think Ian's going to put her with Ten."

He felt his eyes widen. "With Ten? With cold as ice, probably killed someone five minutes ago Ten? I know everyone is claiming that guy is just a friend of Ian's but I swear if he wasn't Special Forces I'll eat my C-leg."

Sean's lips curled up in an enigmatic grin. "I'll get you some sauce to go with that. He's not Special Forces."

"Then he's worse. He's Agency or something. He's not a fucking civilian and he'll hurt her." Ten was also gorgeous and had every sub panting after him. He was ice cold. So cold that the subs were calling him Master No because that was what he said almost all the time. No. He would be so negative around Ally, and that wasn't what she needed. She needed an indulgent Master.

"It doesn't matter what he used to do. Now he's a Dom in training and Ian takes that serious, as you know."

Jake was Macon's mentor. Jake had been disappointed he'd started missing sessions. If he didn't watch it, he would lose his rights in Sanctum altogether, but it didn't really matter. Did it? "Well, I hope that works out for her. I need to hand in my two weeks' notice. I know I'm leaving you in the lurch, but I'm going to move back to New York."

Sean's eyes closed but not before Macon saw a wave of disappointment there. His boss sat back and sighed. "Are you really going to do this?"

Well, he'd known Sean wouldn't be thrilled. "Yes. I think it's time I take my life back."

A chuckle came from Sean's throat but it wasn't an amused sound. He sat back up and gestured to the chair in front of his desk. "Take a seat, Macon."

Macon did as asked. He was sure he was going to get a lecture on how Sean had taken a chance on him—and he had. Getting dressed down by a superior wasn't something Macon liked, but Chef Taggart deserved his pound of flesh. "Of course."

"Are you really so angry that you would go back to a life that you hated?"

"I'm not angry." Why did everyone think he was angry?

"Of course you are. You feel betrayed. She lied to you. Everything life has taught you before this moment tells you to cut her off. Excise the wound and move on. There's only one problem with that. If you excise Allyson from your life, you lose the best part of yourself. You might be angry with her, but are you so angry with yourself you want to self-destruct?"

Before he could even think about it, his hands were fists and they were coming down on Sean's desk with a mighty crack. "I am not fucking angry."

He stared down at the desk. It now had a neat crack that shot up one side. It didn't seem deep but he'd made his presence felt.

Fuck, he was so mad. He was so angry he could barely breathe.

Sean ignored the state of his desk. He turned around a picture frame. It was a shot of Taggart and his wife, Grace, holding their toddler girl with two young men standing behind them. Grace Taggart's children with her first husband. They were all smiling for the camera, but it was easy to see who was the center of attention. Carys Taggart had her mother's coloring but there was no doubt she was a Taggart. "I need you to look at this. This family almost didn't happen because I lied to my wife. I was undercover. I gave her a false name and background and she fell in love with a man who didn't exist. Except I did. I became the man Grace fell in love with. I was better, stronger, more open because of Grace Hawthorne. I lied to her. I nearly cost that woman her life and do you know what she gave me?"

Sean had done those things? He couldn't imagine it. He didn't answer, simply shook his head.

"Forgiveness," Sean said, his voice hitching with emotion. "She gave me forgiveness and a future and then she gave me a family. None of it could have happened without her forgiveness. This little girl doesn't exist without the boundless heart of her mother. Is your frame going to be empty, Macon? Will your anger fill it up or will you simply leave it on a desk utterly devoid of life?"

For the first time since that moment when he realized she'd lied, something cracked inside him. Exactly like that split he'd put in his boss's desk. He could feel the tear.

If he went back to New York, he would lose everything that made him who he was today. He could see his future so clearly. He would work for his father. He could find a society wife who would keep putting off kids until they were too old to have them. He would be trotted out now and again as the war hero, but no one would ask him what he wanted. His future would be set and there wouldn't be a petite sprite of a woman who walked next to him so she could catch him if he fell. Yeah, he knew what she was doing.

"I wouldn't return her calls because I didn't know how to tell her." She wasn't alone in the blame. She shouldn't have lied, but had he forced her hand? "She wanted to know how her brother died and I couldn't tell her. I should never have told her."

Sean got up and walked around the desk, putting a hand on his shoulder. "I've been where the two of you are. I've watched my friends die. I've had to rebuild my life from scratch. And I've had to stand back and pray the only woman I ever loved could find a way to forgive me."

"You never were the reason for your friend's death."

"Of course I was. I was in the military. I had plenty of friends die and I always thought it was my fault."

He didn't understand. "PFC Rowe…"

Sean interrupted. "Took his own life out of either unbearable pain or because he knew you had a better chance without him. We can't know which so give the man the benefit. He was a hero to the end. He sacrificed so you could live. He sacrificed so you could take care of the sister he loved. He might not have known it at the time, but that was how it worked out. You didn't make a mistake by telling her. You made a mistake when you didn't tell his mother."

"I couldn't. How could she not look at me and ask why I didn't spare her son?"

"Maybe, but maybe she would have been proud to raise a child with so much honor. I have a daughter and I want everything in the world for her, but my job as a parent is to raise a good human being. Carla Rowe did that. She seems to have two of them. A woman like that would have seen the beauty in what her son had done. She would have found peace with it. Honor her. Honor him. Find your peace."

He was aware of the tears in his eyes. His father would have told him it wasn't manly, but Sean Taggart squeezed his shoulder. "How do I do that?"

"You talk to Allyson. You give yourself time. You do not go back to a life that you hated. Do you love her?"

That was an easy question to answer. He'd questioned a lot in the last week, but never this. "Yes."

"Do you honestly believe that she loves you?"

A much harder question. It was the one that haunted him, made him surly and angry with everyone around him. "I don't know. I don't see why she would."

"Ask her," Sean urged. "But you have to let go of the past first or you won't believe a word she says. Come to Sanctum with me tonight and talk to her. Tell her you won't allow her to play with Ten."

That was the best idea he'd heard in a long time. "I fucking won't and I'm going to have a talk with Ian. He starts farming my sub out and he won't see another freaking pie again for the rest of his life."

Sean grinned. "I believe you'll discover my brother carefully laid this plan out to get his pie maker back to form. He says your desserts have gone to hell since you broke up with Ally. He can't put his finger on it, but they're missing something."

Macon knew what they were missing. And there was only one way to get it back.

CHAPTER TEN

$\textcircled{M_T}$

Ally burped Kala with a soft pat of her hand against the baby's back. Or was it Kenzie? She gently pulled the baby's left ear back and sure enough there was a tiny mark behind there. Kala. At least Big Tag had switched from a black to a pink Sharpie.

"You doing all right?" Laurel stepped into the room. She was a lovely woman in her late twenties. She looked a little like her brother, Dr. Will Daley. She had a pack of diapers in her hand.

Ally nodded. "They're all sweet kids. I like watching them. It's peaceful."

Laurel's eyes widened. "You're kidding, right? It might seem peaceful now. You wait until Aidan and Tristan fight over a toy. Or Carys. I'm pretty sure those two are actually fighting over Carys. They're like alpha babies. It's weird. I hope Kenzie and Kala don't turn into warrior princesses before my time of servitude is over."

Ally looked at the other woman as she placed Kala in the bassinette she shared with her sleeping sister. The twin girls immediately cuddled up like a pair of puppies and slept. "You don't like kids?"

Laurel reorganized the changing station. "It's not that I don't like them. I'm just pretty sure I won't have them and I'm trying to get to the point that I'm okay with it."

"You can't have kids? You could always adopt." She knew the power of having a loving but non-biological family. Alex and Eve

151

McKay adored their son though he didn't share DNA with either of them.

Laurel sighed. "I'm in love with a man who doesn't want them. Of course he also doesn't want me, so it might be a moot point." Her lips tugged up. "But I'm hopeful. About the wanting me part. He's too stupid to know he wants me yet. I don't think he's going to move on the whole kids thing though. He had a rough childhood and he's the tiniest bit damaged."

God, she knew all about damaged men. "Do you think you can fix him?"

Laurel frowned thoughtfully. "I like him the way he is. That's the crazy part. He's gruff and a control freak and I'm still attracted to him. So I don't necessarily want to fix him. I want him to open up a little so I can see his softer side."

"And if there is no softer side?" Or if his softer side had been locked away forever?

Now Laurel looked sure. "There's always a softer side. Always. My guy's is buried super deep though. But I love him so it's going to be all right, right?"

She wasn't so sure about that. She was proof positive that sometimes love wasn't enough.

Was she really going through with this?

"I heard Master Ian is going to let you work with a Dom tomorrow night," Laurel said as she sat down on the floor. She picked up some blocks and started stacking them, letting the toddlers help her. Sure enough, Tristan was all over Carys and Aidan looked like he wasn't too happy about it. "Are you nervous? I heard it's the new guy. I've worked with some of the married Doms. They rotate in and out until they decide we're ready to mix with the singles. At least that's what they tell me. I suspect someone is pulling the strings and keeping me away from the single guys. I think it's either my brother or my boss."

She found the other sub trainee's lives endlessly entertaining. "Your brother and your boss are both Sanctum members?"

"Yeah," Laurel admitted. "It can get weird at times. My sister-in-law is cool, but Will claims Lisa and I are going to make him go blind."

"And your boss? Is it weird to see him here?"

Laurel kind of sighed. "I haven't actually seen him here. I'm not entirely sure he even knows I joined. I'm afraid to bring up the subject. I train on Thursdays. He never comes in on Thursdays. I really want to see him in his leathers."

"Oh, so he's the one who doesn't want kids."

A faint tinge of red flushed her cheeks. "Mitch has a very skewed view of the world. He's been married a couple of times, and to say they didn't go well would be like saying Pompeii was a just a little explosion. So I think he likes me, but he's leery of getting involved with anyone. From what I can tell, all his very short-term relationships happen here at Sanctum."

And now Laurel was here at Sanctum, prepared to force her man to make the choice to watch her go to another Dom or take her for himself. "Wow. Even I know that's topping from the bottom."

Laurel smiled. "I know. Smart, right?"

Wasn't that what she was doing? Ally told herself this was all about finding herself and she meant it. Besides, Macon had asked her to leave. She'd packed her crappy belongings and was staying on Deena's couch until she could find a place of her own. But she wasn't going to let him shove her out of Top or Sanctum. The question was would she want to be here without him?

Ally wasn't so sure. She also wasn't so sure about the man Master Ian called Ten. She'd met him earlier and while the man was past gorgeous, he'd also seemed cold. Even when he'd smiled and called her "darlin'" in a slow Southern accent, she'd felt a chill from him.

But she was going to trust Master Ian. Macon had shown her this world and she liked it. Just because he no longer wanted her didn't mean someone out there wouldn't. And if he came back, she would know more than she'd known before. She'd looked over the training contract and there was a strict no-sex policy until Master Ian and Master Kai were sure she was here for the right reasons.

That clause in her contract had given her security. She could breathe easy. She had her safe word. She had her contract. She had mentor Doms and subs who would look out for her.

She simply didn't have her Master anymore.

The door came open and Lisa poked her head in. "Ally, tap out and get into the kitchen. Serious drama going on. Master Macon showed up with Master Sean and he's yelling at everyone. I mean everyone. He's especially pissy with Master No. I mean Master T. Don't tell anyone I called him that. We all get spanked when we call him that and not the fun kind of spanking."

Macon was here and he was going after her training Dom? Ally raced down the hall, secure that Lisa and Laurel could handle the kiddos. What was Macon thinking? Fighting another Dom could get him kicked out. And why would he care? He'd made himself plain earlier in the day.

She passed through the back of the house, managing to avoid the larger areas where the scenes would play out. Even from the hall she could hear Macon.

"I swear to god you touch my sub and we're going to have trouble."

"I was unaware she was your sub," came that sexy voice that belonged to Master T. "She sure isn't wearing a collar now, is she?"

"I'm warning you," Macon said as she entered the kitchen. His back was to her, but she could see his threats hadn't made a dent in Master T's demeanor.

The big Southern Master stood beside Master Ian while Master Sean was beside Macon. The tension was so thick she couldn't breathe.

Ally was about to speak when she felt a hand on her shoulder.

"Don't say a word. This is what I like to call a Dom Standoff." Charlotte Taggart sounded genuinely amused. "Watch them. They'll get the ruler out soon and compare dick sizes. I turned down the air conditioner just in case. It'll be icy cold in here soon."

Macon had realized she was in the room and was frowning her way. "Go back to the daycare, Allyson. I'll come and get you in a moment."

He thought he could boss her around now? "Uhm, Master T is right. I'm not wearing your collar, Macon. You kicked me out so I don't have to do anything you say."

Master T smiled, though it was really more of a smirk. "That's right, darlin'. You give him hell. I picked out a sweet training collar for you. Why don't we go somewhere private and see if it fits."

Before Master T could say another word, Master Ian's fist came out and popped him right in the nose.

Master T groaned but rolled his eyes and strode across to the fridge. "You know, Ian, one of these days you're going to run out of those."

Ally was fairly certain they were all insane.

"Ten, I told you not to fuck with the pie maker. You're about to give him a heart attack. Do you see that tic over his left eye? I can't lose the pie maker," Ian explained. He turned to Ally. "You want to fix him?"

Macon was staring at her. "Come here, Ally."

Did she want to fix him? Yes. Did he want to be fixed? She wasn't so sure about that.

"Go on. He's on the edge," Charlotte whispered in her ear. "He can go one of two ways. You fight him and he'll probably go insane. But if you submit, I think he won't be able to help himself. Your choice, Ally. Decide if you want him right now."

There was no decision to be made. She walked to him and then pointedly chose his right side. She sank to her knees, clinging to his damaged leg. She needed him to know that she loved every part of him.

His hand came down and she felt him sigh. His palm covered her scalp. "Master Ian, I know I'm still in training, but I would prefer you didn't pawn off my submissive to other Doms."

Master Ian gave him a thumbs-up. "Done. She's all yours, buddy."

"So I take it you won't be heading back to New York," Master Sean said and then whistled. "Wow, I think my brother loves you. He just went pale at the very thought of you leaving."

Charlotte took her husband's hand. "Come on, baby. Let's get you a drink. I know this breakup has been rough on you, but it's all right now. The pie guy is staying. Right?"

There was a definite "or else" to Charlotte's tone.

"I'm staying, but I need to talk to Allyson alone." Macon's hand stroked her hair.

"Use one of the guest rooms. They're set up as privacy rooms for the evening," Charlotte explained. "Come on, Ten. I'll get you a drink, too, and we'll find you a girl to spank tomorrow."

"Laurel. I think he should definitely work with Laurel." Ally offered up her new friend. Hey, the threat of being with Master No seemed to have worked for her.

Ian Taggart got to one knee. He was a big, gorgeous beast of a man. "You wouldn't happen to be attempting to help Laurel make Mitchell Bradford jealous, would you?"

He was also intimidating as hell. The hand on her head stroked, letting her know Macon would protect her. "I only know Laurel is very ready to start her journey, Sir."

One side of Big Tag's mouth tugged up. "I like the way you think, mini pie maker. You two should fuck regularly and have a bunch of pie-making babies." He stood up. "Ten, let's go introduce you to Laurel."

"Am I going to get punched again?" he asked, his voice tight.

"Not by me, buddy. I'm hoarding mine."

"Yeah, well, you seem to find a ton of ways around those rules, asshole," Master T was saying as they left the room.

"I'm going to find my wife," Chef Taggart said. "See you two for dinner service tomorrow."

The kitchen was suddenly quiet, though she could hear the low thud of music coming from the front of the house. She was alone with Macon and she had to wonder if he'd only been jealous and if they wouldn't be right back where they'd started.

"Come on, baby." His voice was harsh as though he'd been screaming at someone and it had hurt his vocal chords.

She glanced up and he was reaching down to help her. She got to her feet and he started to lead her away. He didn't say anything else, merely led her through the hallway and down to a room she hadn't been in before. He turned on the light and she could see it was a small guestroom with a queen-sized bed. It would have been a perfectly normal room except for the spanking bench to the side of the bed and the hooks hanging from the ceiling. She was fairly certain there would be instruments of erotic torture in the closet.

What did Macon want to say to her? Was he already regretting the scene he'd caused?

The minute the door was closed, he was on her. He dragged her close and his mouth devoured hers. "Please forgive me."

"Macon? What are you talking about? I need you to forgive me."

His head shook even as he kept his forehead against hers. "I pushed you to it. I wouldn't talk to you because I thought it should have been me. I was ashamed."

Her heart ached for him. "Never. You survived. I love you. I love you so much. I never want to hear you say that again."

"I've been angry, Ally. I think I've been angry most of my life and I wouldn't admit it. I was so mad at you. Hell, I was mad at Adam and I finally figured out why." He tugged at her shirt, dragging it up and over her head. His hands went straight to her bra, undoing the fasteners and pulling it off.

"Why?" She was compliant, allowing him to do the work he seemed to need. If he wanted her naked, she could do that for him. "Adam simply told you the truth."

"Because if he'd waited a couple of days we would have been

married and I wouldn't have been able to shove you aside. I would have been forced to deal with you. I was so mad he couldn't have waited a couple of days."

She sighed, reaching up to touch his face. "Baby, it's better this way. It's better to start our lives together honestly. I can see that now. I wanted you too badly to risk losing you. You're everything I could have hoped for."

"How do you do that to me? I've got nothing right now. I used to have money and a career that I trained my whole life for. I used to be whole, but somehow when you look at me like you're doing now—I'm more than I was. I'm greater than I used to be. How is that possible?"

"I don't know, but I feel the same and I don't want to lose it."

He crowded her, moving her toward the bed until the backs of her legs hit the side. "Marry me."

"Yes." She would never say no to him when it came to being together. He was arrogant and hardheaded at times, but she belonged with him.

He pushed at her jeans and she helped him this time, shoving them over her thighs and dragging her panties with them. She kicked off her sandals and she was naked before him.

"And you won't be playing with that Southern dickwad," he proclaimed.

"I wasn't ever going to play with him. I was going to let him train with me," she corrected.

"Spanking bench. Now."

Shit. She should have known he was going to want his discipline time. She definitely knew better than to argue with the Dom. Macon's shoulders had straightened, his voice deepening despite the hoarseness there. He was moving into Master mode and he was hungry for some play.

She looked at the contraption and cursed Ian Taggart for having such a well stocked home. She was likely going to be sore tomorrow.

And she would love it. She would stretch and feel that little ache and remember how close they'd gotten, how much she'd pleased her Master and he'd pleased her.

With only a bit of awkwardness, she managed to mold her body to the spanking bench. It placed her ass high in the air, gave her a padded resting place for her shins and forearms but allowed her breasts to dangle. All in all, as torture devices went, it was pretty dang comfy.

"I want one of these. Look at that." He was standing behind her, studying her ass, and it was obvious he liked what he saw. "This is awfully convenient."

His big palms cupped her cheeks.

She breathed, dragging air into her lungs because her body was already preparing for him. "What am I being punished for, Master? The lie?"

His hand stilled. "No. I forgive you for the lie if you forgive me for ignoring your very reasonable requests. I'm so sorry for that."

He'd been scared. So had she. "You're forgiven, babe. Both of those actions brought us here, so I wouldn't take either one back."

"You're being punished for bringing that man between us. Never again, Allyson."

"I thought you were leaving," she pointed out. It was good to know he could get jealous, too.

"I thought I was, too, but now I can clearly see that had more to do with me than you, baby." His fingers ran up the length of her spine. "I think I would have come back. I don't know how long it would have taken, but I would have come back to you after I pulled my head out of my ass. Would I have found you with that asshole Dom?"

Oh, he had it bad. "I'll get you a copy of my contract."

"You signed a fucking contract with him?" He knelt down beside her, his eyes flaring. Yep, Macon was letting his anger flow. She wouldn't be surprised if the man didn't go all green and Hulky on her.

So she decided to stay calm and pleasant. "I did. I signed an ironclad contract stating I wouldn't have sex with the man and no intimate touching."

He sighed and stood again. "So he gets to live. Let's never do this again, Allyson. My heart can't take it. Big Tag was right. I can feel my blood pressure ticking up. I can only think of one way to relax again."

She could imagine what that was. And then she didn't have to imagine because a loud smack filled the room. Her backside lit up and her whole body seemed braced for the storm.

"No matter what happens, you can't put another man between us." He slapped her ass again and again.

Though she knew he was angry, every smack was controlled. He didn't hit the same place twice and every bit of the slight pain he gave her morphed into heat and anticipation.

"I will never walk out on you again, Ally. I swear that to you." He spanked her again, but he was slowing down. Each smack was punctuated with a caress. His free hand moved to her pussy, sliding through her ever more aroused female parts. "We can fight it out, but I won't leave you and I won't be such a massive tool."

She had to smile. He was educable. "You were an asshole this morning."

He lifted her off the bench in a show of strength that made her gasp. Before she could protest, he tossed her on the bed. "I was. I'm sorry, baby. I was such a jerk that I didn't even taste your pie or anything you made me. Will you bake for me again?"

"You're the chef, Macon. I was only trying stuff out."

"From my mom's book."

She nodded. "It made me feel close to you."

He pulled his shirt over his head and tossed it aside. "Let's try them all out together. Since I started working at Top, I've been dealing with much more complex recipes, but I want to make everything my mom made. I want to do that with you."

She nodded. "I will. Come here, Master. I need you."

He got out of his jeans and then sat on the bed, pulling his artificial leg off with a sigh. She got on her knees and watched him. She had no idea how the world had handled him when he was in one piece because the "damaged" version of Macon was almost too beautiful to look at.

"Only you, baby. Only you can make me feel this way." He turned, catching her and flipping them both over. "I want to give Tristan a cousin. I want every tie I can have with you."

She wasn't getting any younger and neither was he. She wanted that family she saw at night in her dreams. "Yes, Master."

He was on top of her, separating her legs and fitting himself to her. "I like the sound of that. I love that you're my submissive, but I think I'll like calling you my wife even more."

His hips thrust up, joining them. She was slick and wet, receiving him as easily as she could. He was so big inside. Her man filled her up and she loved how she had to wriggle to truly take him. She wrapped her legs around him as he thrust up, impaling her on his cock. He stopped and gave her a moment to get used to him.

"I missed you. I missed this so much." He lay on top of her, giving her every delicious ounce of his weight.

"I was so lonely without you." Years she'd spent alone, but it was only when this man left her that she'd truly understood how empty she could feel.

"You feel so good. So right. Nothing ever felt as right as being inside you." He held himself still against her, taking her mouth under his. His tongue plunged in a show of what was to come.

Slowly, his hips began to move. They found the rhythm his tongue set before he broke off the kiss and rose above her.

"I'll never get tired of watching you come. Come for me, baby. I want to watch you light up." He thrust in harder and faster, his pelvis grinding against her clit. His cock moved inside, searching until he found the right spot.

Ally felt her eyes widen and she didn't try to stop the shout that came from her throat as Macon's cock glided over that perfect spot and she came. The world seemed to fall away and there was only pleasure. She moved with him, trying to get every drop of sensation to be had.

Macon watched her, his eyes holding hers until his body stiffened and he thrust in short strokes. His head fell forward as he fucked her hard and then ground down. She could feel heat flowing from him to her.

He sagged against her, but kept them connected as though he couldn't stand the thought of not being inside her. He buried his face against her neck as Ally let the sweetness of afterglow flow across her.

"Do you know how beautiful you are?" His hoarse voice got to her.

"I only feel this way around you." She smoothed his hair back, reveling in the fact that this big gorgeous man was all hers. She had to ask him about that rasp though. "What happened to your voice?"

He cupped her face, kissing her forehead like she was something to be worshipped. "I finally cried, baby. I finally let it out. I don't know that I'm through. I'm still angry about a lot of things, but I know that you're the best thing that ever happened to me."

She held on to him. "I'll help you. We might not have a lot, but we've got each other, baby."

"Yes, a place to stay, a car, and three and a quarter legs," he whispered against her skin. He chuckled. "We've got it all."

Maybe not all, but it was more than enough to build a future on.

AUTHOR'S NOTE

I'm often asked by generous readers how they can help get the word out about a book they enjoyed. There are so many ways to help an author you like. Leave a review. If your e-reader allows you to lend a book to a friend, please share it. Go to Goodreads and connect with others. Recommend the books you love because stories are meant to be shared. Thank you so much for reading this book and for supporting all the authors you love!

MASTER NO
Masters and Mercenaries, Book 9
By Lexi Blake
Coming August 4, 2015

Disavowed by those he swore to protect…

Tennessee Smith is a wanted man. Betrayed by his government and hunted by his former employer, he's been stripped of everything he holds dear. If the CIA finds him, they're sure to take his life as well. His only shot at getting it all back is taking down the man who burned him. He knows just how to get to Senator Hank McDonald and that's through his daughter, Faith. In order to seduce her, he must become something he never thought he'd be—a Dom.

Overcome by isolation and duty…

All her life, Dr. Faith "Mac" McDonald has felt alone, even among her family. Dedicating herself to helping others and making a difference in the world has brought her some peace, but a year spent fighting the Ebola virus in West Africa has taken a toll. She's come home for two months of relaxation before she goes back into the field. After holding so many lives in her hands, nothing restores her like the act of submission. Returning to her favorite club, Mac is drawn to the mysterious new Dom all the subs are talking about, Master No. In the safety of his arms, she finds herself falling head over heels in love.

Forced to choose between love and revenge…

On an exclusive Caribbean island, Ten and Mac explore their mutual attraction, but her father's plots run deeper than Ten could possibly have imagined. With McKay-Taggart by his side, Ten searches for a way to stop the senator, even as his feelings for Mac become too strong to deny. In the end, he must choose between love and revenge—a choice that will change his life forever.

* * * *

"Do they really call you Master No?"

He chuckled. "Apparently. But you're not going to call me that. Are you?"

He was right back to staring at her lips. Actually, it was nice to see the horny side of Tennessee. She loved his name. It fit the man. Enigmatic. "Why do they call you that?"

He scooted closer to her, so close their chests almost touched. "Because I don't play around. Not with women who don't mean something to me. I have my duties at Sanctum and I fulfill them, but I'm not indulgent with women who don't belong to me. I tend to be very much the opposite."

Another thing she didn't understand. Even in their texts and Internet conversations, he'd been indulgent with her. He seemed to want to see her do things that pleased her. He'd ordered her to eat chocolate one night when she said she shouldn't because she was worried about her weight. She did not make that mistake twice. He'd watched as she'd had her first real chocolate in almost a year. "You're not that way with me."

"I have a contract that states very plainly you do belong to me." He stared at her for a moment and she had an unnerving thought that he could see right through her. "You're not afraid of what could happen to you after yesterday. You're afraid of what could happen between the two of us."

Well, he wasn't pussyfooting around the situation. "Like I said, it feels different than I thought it would. I feel more than I thought I would."

He moved in again and she could suddenly feel his heat all over. Not just his heat. Something really big and really hard was resting against her thigh. It was fairly close to where it should be. Could be. Might be soon.

"There's nothing wrong with that, Faith. Did you really want to sleep with a man you didn't know?"

That three weeks had been the difference. She supposed she'd expected they would get in touch but not a lot more. They would come together to play and have sex. It felt like more than sex. Being so close to Tennessee felt more intimate than actually having sex with Roger. "No. I thought I did. I thought it was kind of the right thing to do. Real' relationships are hard for me. My career is kind of demanding."

His fingertips brushed over her collarbone. God, he was killing her. "Yes, it's demanding, but you know what I think?"

164

He leaned over and kissed the tip of her nose, a sweet gesture.

He was being so tender with her and she wanted to scream at him to just jump on her and have his wicked way. Her body was getting primed. Her nipples were so hard. They might climb off her body and try to get between his ridiculously sexy lips. "I don't. I don't know anything right now."

Except the fact that she wanted him. It was probably a bad idea, but she wanted him.

"Then let me help you out, darlin'. You don't have to think for a while. Let's both stop thinking and follow our instincts for once." He moved in and his lips caressed hers.

Easy, thoughtful, at first he simply pressed his mouth to hers, letting them rub together as though taking stock of the feel of her. Ten didn't overwhelm her. He started slow. He let her sigh against him as he brushed his lips over hers and let her taste the mint on his mouth.

She gasped and pushed against him. "You already got up and brushed your teeth."

The most devilish look went over his face and he stopped playing. He rolled over and his body was on top of hers, his hips coaxing her legs to open wide. Before she really knew what he was doing, his cock was right on her core. "Yes, I did. I woke up and I showered and brushed my teeth, and my poor little sub slept the morning away. I came back out here and climbed into bed with you and waited for my moment. I'm going to eat you up, Faith."

His mouth covered hers and she couldn't fight him. It felt too good. His tongue surged and he seemed eager to devour her. His mouth slanted over hers again and again, his body heavy but in the best of ways. She loved his weight bearing her down into the mattress. There really wasn't enough space for the two of them, but they didn't need it. They simply nestled together until she wasn't sure how to untangle their limbs. His chest pressed down, warmth flaring through her as his tongue invaded.

He'd gotten up and prepared himself for her. Oh, he wasn't giving her the same courtesy, but he didn't seem to need it. He wasn't acting like a man who wasn't enjoying himself.

"Stop thinking, Faith," he growled against her lips. "You taste good. You're fucking perfect and I dreamed about doing this all night. Best dreams I've had in forever. I'm not waiting for you to decide you're good enough for me. I'm telling you. You're perfect and I want to fuck you more than I want my next damn breath."

He took her mouth before she could respond and she just kind of melted under him. There was nothing else to do. He'd taken control and she needed this.

He kissed her and his hands explored, running under her tank top and up to the under curve of her breast. His cock was suddenly right on top of her mound. Only her pajama bottoms, thin undies, and his boxers were between them. She could feel the hard line of his erection jutting between her thighs, dragging over her pussy in a blatant imitation of what he would do once he got inside her.

"Dreamed about this all damn night." He shifted off to the side and his hand suddenly cupped her, one thumb brushing over her nipple. "Hell, I've dreamed about this since we started talking, Faith, and I think you have, too. That's why you're acting so skittish this morning. You like me."

So arrogant and so damn right. She couldn't help but smile at him. "I do. I like you a lot, Tennessee."

He rolled her nipple between his thumb and forefinger. "Well, that's a good thing because I like you, too, Faith."

SCANDAL NEVER SLEEPS
The Perfect Gentlemen, Book 1
By Shayla Black and Lexi Blake
Coming August 18, 2015

They are the Perfect Gentlemen of Creighton Academy: privileged, wealthy, powerful friends with a wild side. But a deadly scandal is about to tear down their seemingly ideal lives...

Maddox Crawford's sudden death sends Gabriel Bond reeling. Not only is he burying his best friend, he's cleaning up Mad's messes, including his troubled company. Grieving and restless, Gabe escapes his worries in the arms of a beautiful stranger. But his mind-blowing one-night stand is about to come back to haunt him . . .

Mad groomed Everly Parker to be a rising star in the executive world. Now that he's gone, she's sure her job will be the next thing she mourns, especially after she ends up accidentally sleeping with her new boss. If only their night together hadn't been so incendiary—or Gabe like a fantasy come true...

As Gabe and Everly struggle to control the heated tension between them, they discover evidence that Mad's death was no accident. Now they must bank their smoldering passions to hunt down a murderer—because Mad had secrets that someone was willing to kill for, and Gabe or Everly could be the next target...

* * * *

"I want to see you."

Even in the low light, he noticed her breath hitch. "You want me to turn on the lights?"

"That's not what I meant." He never took his burning gaze from her. "I want to see you naked. Take off your dress. Show me your breasts."

"I'll close the curtains." She started to turn to the windows.

He caught her elbow, gently restraining her. "Don't. We're high up. No one can see in. Take off your dress. Let me see you in the moonlight."

Her gaze tangled with his, and he could see a hint of her trepidation. A gentleman might have backed down. But he knew what he wanted. She must want him too or she wouldn't have agreed to spend the night with him. He wasn't giving Eve the easy way out.

Finally, she turned her back to him and lifted her arms, struggling to reach the metal tab. "There's a zipper down the back."

He moved closer. "Let me."

Gabe ran his hands up her spine before finding the zipper. She lifted her curls out of his way, exposing the graceful column of her neck. Her skin looked pale, almost incandescent in the low light. He couldn't help himself. He leaned over and kissed her nape, feeling her shiver under his touch.

Slowly, he eased the zipper down, his fingertips brushing her spine. Once he passed her neck, she let her hair fall free, the strawberry-blond mass tumbling well past her shoulders, gliding over her skin. Her tresses were soft, too. Not severely flat-ironed. Different, like the woman herself. Fuck, he could lose himself in Eve.

She shrugged, allowing the straps of her dress to fall past her shoulders and drop to her waist.

Her bra looked plain and white. He was used to delicate garments meant to entice a man, so he had no idea why the site of her utilitarian bra made his cock jerk. She hadn't been seeking a man this evening, much less intending to seduce a lover. When she'd dressed, it had been for comfort. But now, she was here with him, slowly peeling away her clothes.

With practiced ease, he unhooked her bra with a twist of his hand and slid his fingers under the straps to strip them off. He closed his eyes and allowed his hands to roam across the wealth of smooth skin he'd just exposed. He drew her back against his chest and grazed his way up her abdomen until he found her breasts. Full and real, he loved the weight of them in his palms. He drew his thumbs over the nubs of her nipples and Eve rewarded him with a long intake of breath.

"That feels so good." As she leaned back against him for support, she shuddered and thrust her breasts up like twin offerings.

He would absolutely take everything she had to give.

Gabe filled his hands with her flesh, cupping and rubbing and discovering every inch of her breasts before he grew impatient to have her totally bare and pushed the dress over the curve of her hips. It pooled on the floor at her feet.

Her underwear matched her bra. If she were his, he would buy her La Perla. He would dress her like a goddess in silk and lace and know that she wore the most come-hither lingerie for his eyes only. She could wear her ladylike dresses and cover herself with all appropriate modesty if she wanted—but only until they were alone.

As he stripped off her panties, a wild possessiveness blazed through his system. Gabe turned her to face him, well aware that he needed to slow down but utterly incapable of doing so. He took in the sight of her breasts. They looked every bit as perfect as they'd felt.

"You're beautiful."

"I don't feel that way." She tilted her face up to his, drinking him in with her stare. There was nothing coy about her expression. She looked at him with naked yearning. "Not most of the time. But you make me feel sexy."

"You are. I want to be very clear about how beautiful I think you are." He kissed her again, lifting her up and out of her dress, heading back to the bedroom while his mouth ate hungrily at hers.

She didn't fight him, didn't fidget to make him set her back on the ground. She simply wrapped her arms around his neck and let him carry her. Her fingers sank into his hair and she held tight while her tongue danced against his.

Luckily, he knew Plaza suites like the back of his hand. He maneuvered her toward the bed, his cock throbbing insistently.

He wouldn't last long. God, he couldn't believe he was even thinking that. Usually, he could go for hours, but Gabe knew the minute he got inside Eve, he was going to lose control. He needed to make it good for her now because he'd barely touched her and already he wanted to throw her against the wall and shove his way inside her.

As he approached the mattress, he stopped and eased her onto the luxurious comforter. She lay back on the elegant duvet, her hair fanned out and her legs spread. Wanton and yet so innocent. He pulled at his shirt, hearing a button or two pop off, but at the moment he didn't give a shit. The need to be skin to skin with her drove him to haste. He unbuckled his belt and shoved his pants down.

"Foreplay." Freaking hell. He was so ready to go, he'd forgotten about that. Women liked foreplay. It tended to be necessary for them.

She shook her head. "The kissing was foreplay. We're totally good."

Shit. He had to slow down. He wasn't exactly a small guy. She needed to be ready to take all of him.

Gabe took a deep breath. "Need you aroused. It's okay. Just give me a minute."

"Gabriel, I am as aroused as I have ever been in my life. I'm a little worried about what kind of stain I'm going to leave for the staff on this duvet. So really, can we get this train moving?"

He gripped her ankles and slid her down the bed, spreading her legs wider in the process. His cock twitched when he saw that she was right. Her pussy was wet. Juicy. He could see its slick gloss from above, even in the shadows. A little kissing, some groping, and she was ready to go. He'd never had a woman respond to him so readily. "Tell me again."

"I'm ready," she vowed. "I am really ready."

"No, tell me this isn't normal for you," he corrected. It was stupid. She was right there, able and willing to give him the pleasure he sought—but he craved more. He needed to know that tonight was special for her. "Tell me you want me and not just sex."

She gave him a sheepish smile. "This isn't at all normal. I guess I've gone a little crazy tonight, but I don't do one-night stands. I can count the men I've had sex with on one hand and I wouldn't need all my fingers. And I've never, never wanted anyone as much as I want you right now. Gabriel, I don't need foreplay, just you."

ABOUT LEXI BLAKE

Lexi Blake lives in North Texas with her husband, three kids, and the laziest rescue dog in the world. She began writing at a young age, concentrating on plays and journalism. It wasn't until she started writing romance that she found success. She likes to find humor in the strangest places. Lexi believes in happy endings no matter how odd the couple, threesome or foursome may seem. She also writes contemporary Western ménage as Sophie Oak.

Connect with Lexi online:

Facebook: www.facebook.com/lexi.blake.39
Twitter: https://twitter.com/authorlexiblake
Website: www.LexiBlake.net

Sign up for Lexi's free newsletter at www.lexiblake.net/contact

23269655R00110

Made in the USA
Middletown, DE
20 August 2015